Mine to Treasure

Veteran K9 Team
Book 8

Kameron Claire

Snuggle Whore Press, LLC

Dedication

This series is dedicated to every individual
who signs a blank check on their ass
by enlisting in the Armed Forces
to serve their country—and to the
loved ones who support them back home.

We are Witty, Wicked & Wild wherever we go!

VETERAN
K9
TEAM
REPORTING
FOR DUTY

Chapter 1
Prologue - Saint

Ten Years Ago...

After six months of boot camp and advanced training, I'm finally free to join the Rangers unit as one of their dozen K9 handlers. I've been in Georgia for the better half of a year, and this will be home base when we aren't deployed. Honestly, I'm ready to start the next phase of my life, get on a plane, and go to parts unknown.

No more tedious training—although, let's be honest, Hades and I will train together until one or both of us end up in a pine box or retired.

It's morbid, but it's true.

Now that I'm assigned to the Ranger battalion—a unit I fought hard to get into—I'm ready to cut loose and have some fun before we deploy. Who knows when the next opportunity to get laid will come?

It's now or never, soldier.

My sponsor, Sergeant John Vale, texts me.

Get your ass to Hooligans ASAP. Here's the address.

A pinned location pops up on my phone.

Be there in twenty. I reply before jumping in the shower.

Hooligans is a private club for Ranger battalion members and their guests. That's the only reason my eighteen-year-old ass can enter, because as of today, I'm attached to their infamous unit. Guilt and glory by association, and far easier than training to become an actual Ranger.

I walk into the place with way too much big dick energy considering the men assembled and instantly remind myself to tone it down. No reason to get my ass beat on Day One. Still, I'm eighteen, horny, and feeling invincible considering this is the best day of my life.

Sergeant Vale, whom I met briefly when I brought Hades over from the training facility to meet the other dogs this morning, raises his beer and calls me over. He glances at his watch. "Two minutes to spare."

Punctuality is a thing with these guys as it is a simple form of discipline. One of many things I will have to learn while on the job, my training to-date only taking me so far amongst these elite warfighters.

He motions to the guy standing next to him. "This is Sergeant Kemp. He's also a handler and one of the team leads."

"Sergeant." I offer my hand.

He shakes it. "Inside these walls you can call me Kemp."

"And you call me Vale." John offers me a beer.

"Am I allowed to drink this?" I eye the frosty bottle, my throat suddenly parched. I've been drinking domestic shit beer since I was four. It's practically water to me. My father's an alcoholic, as was my mother before she died of cancer nine months ago, so I come by it honestly. Of course, my tolerance is way higher than the average eighteen-year-old, but this feels like a test that I have no intention of failing.

"Inside these walls or the privacy of your room, sure. But no driving and no brawls. Nothing to get unwanted attention, especially from the MPs or the local LE." He pushes it into my hand.

"Thanks." I take a swig and look around. "So everyone in here is Ranger battalion?"

"Or invited guest." Kemp eyes me, as if he's waiting for me to say or do something stupid.

"Even the women?"

Vale chuckles and shakes his head. "Been a long time, sailor?"

I sigh and take another swig. "You remember how the last couple of weeks of training are. I haven't been able to roam free for over a month."

"Most of the women around here know they have an open invitation to this establishment, even if it is private. So, no. Not all the women in here are attached."

I nod, my eyes scanning the bar and locking on to a set of four ladies near the digital jukebox, one woman standing out. Beautiful, she's short and muscular with just the right amount of curve gripping her well-worn jeans. She wears her T-shirt tight across her B-cups, which makes me wish a frigid chill would blow through the room. Blonde hair cut into a short bob, cute button nose, sparkly blue-green eyes complete the package. And freckles. With her complexion, I bet if I got closer I'd discover she has freckles—which are my weakness. "Do either of you know the blonde?"

Vale and Kemp exchange a look, which should have been my first clue. "We've seen her around a few times."

"Do you think she's hooked up with any of these guys?" My mouth runs on autopilot, my brain and dick focused on one thing.

"I'm positive she's not," Kemp says.

"As a matter of fact, she's kind of a ball buster. I don't think I've ever seen her dance with a guy, much less go home with him," Vale adds.

"Maybe she hasn't had the right guy ask her." Kemp tips his bottle back and drains the contents.

Vale grins and elbows me playfully. "You should go ask her. Maybe a young stud like you can get her to say yes."

I roll my eyes. "You guys are setting me up."

Kemp chuckles. "Why would you say that?"

Shaking my head, I finish my beer faster than I probably should in front of my new team leads. "I don't know, but this feels like a setup."

Vale hands me two beers out of an ice bucket. "Maybe we want to see her knock you down a couple pegs."

"Or maybe we want to see what kind of stud you really are." Kemp clinks his fresh bottle to mine.

I narrow my eyes and then look her way again to find her staring at us.

No, not us. Me.

"Are you sure you're not trying to get my ass kicked?"

Kemp's face gets serious. "We wouldn't do that. You get into a fight, then we have to get into a fight, and I have no desire to tangle with any of the motherfuckers in here."

"Truth," Vale adds.

Sighing, I watch her as she stares at me with keen interest.

Fuck it. These guys are up to something, but she's more than interested in what I'm putting out, and no man ever died from rejection.

I stroll across the small space, put the two beers down on the table, and pull my billfold out of my pocket, feigning interest in the jukebox. "Do you mind if I play a couple of songs?"

"Be my guest." The blonde says with a small tilt to her perfectly pouty lips. One look at her up close and the other three women fade away.

Fuck, I was right. Freckles!

I swear my cock just jumped to attention to salute her.

"What can I play you?" I say without taking my eyes off the screen.

"What makes you think I like music?" She cocks her

hip and leans against the wall, taking the beer I offer without words ever being exchanged.

"Well, you've been standing here for fifteen minutes reviewing the selection. That gives me a small clue."

She smiles casually. "I like all kinds of music."

"Which song do you want to dance to?" I flash her my smoothest smile—the one that made all the girls' panties drop in high school.

Freckles arches her brow as if she's unimpressed. "Are you asking me to dance?"

I double down. "We can start with a dance and see where the night takes us."

Her grin turns knowing. Well, at least she's amused by my dumb ass. "Aren't you a cocky one?"

"Not cocky. Confident. I thought women like confident men?"

"Only when you can back it up."

"Dance with me and find out."

She glances around the private club. "If you haven't noticed, this isn't much of a dancing establishment."

I also glance around. It's a Wednesday afternoon, just after seven pm, so there are only a dozen people here. "That's dumb. What better way is there to get a beautiful woman into your arms and pull her so close that not even a piece of paper separates you?"

"A piece of paper? Like a marriage certificate?" She taunts.

I quickly glance at her hands. "Oh shit. You're not married, are you?"

Chuckling, she shakes her head. "No, I'm not."

"Whew. I don't want to be that guy." I pick up my beer and take a drink.

Her bottle is balanced delicately between two fingers, inches from her mouth, as if she's sizing me up and deciding if she needs to quench her thirst or not. I would love to make her thirsty—for me. "If I was married, I should be here with my husband or not at all, don't you think?"

I shake my head. "No. I think a married woman can and should go out with her girlfriends. And as long as she's honest about her relationship, she should expect any man who approaches her to respect her commitment."

She presses her lips together and nods slowly. "Good answer."

"Good enough to give me your name?"

"Janey."

I offer her my hand. "Saint."

Her eyes narrow, but she shakes my hand, anyway. "Are you giving me a fake name?"

"No, my last name is Santiago but my family has called me Saint since I was a baby. I have a little sister I call Demon." I flash her a grin. "And now a dog named Hades."

"A dog? Let me guess. She's a fluffy little Shih Tzu."

"No, but if there was ever an appropriate pet name for a breed of dog, I'm thinking a demon's name works."

"Shih Tzu or a Chihuahua." She smiles, and this one touches her eyes.

Damn. I like this woman. She's smart, confident, and fuck me—those freckles.

"Let me take you out on a date."

She shakes her head. "Don't you think I'm a little old for you?"

"No. I'm thinking you're maybe two to three years older than me, but what I lack in age, I make up for in experience."

"Oh, really?"

"Oh yeah, baby."

She shakes her head and suppresses her smile before tilting her head over my shoulder. "Your friends over there. Did they put you up to this?"

I glance over my shoulder at Vale and Kemp, who have all of their attention trained on us with shit-eating grins on their faces. "Something tells me they're setting me up, but you're worth it."

"Do you think so?"

"Yeah. I do."

She downs the rest of the bottle quickly and hands me the empty. "Well, Saint, it was very entertaining meeting you, but I have an early morning and need to get home. Maybe I'll see you around."

"Wait." I put my hand out but don't touch her. Something tells me she wouldn't find that cute in the slightest. "Won't you at least give me your number?"

She looks me up and down slowly, her eyes finally coming back to mine. "I tell you what. The next time we see each other, if you still want it, ask me then."

She's challenging me, and I'm up for it. "I'll do that."

"We'll see." She steps around me and walks right up to Vale and Kemp, saying something low enough that I can't hear. It's only a couple of words, and she doesn't give either of them a chance to respond before turning and walking away. Once she's at the door, she looks over her shoulder and flashes me a smile, and then my dream girl is gone.

Damn. I'm going to like being out in the world.

VETERAN
K9
TEAM
REPORTING
FOR DUTY

Chapter 2
Prologue Continued - Janey

The next morning, Gwar and I are in the office early. Sergeant First Class Barron Theroux is out for the next two weeks and put me in charge in his absence. Even though I only outrank Vale and Kemp by a couple of weeks' time in grade, I think I'd be in charge no matter what. I'm way more mature than either of those two jackasses, who I will make pay today for the shenanigans they pulled last night.

Sending the new guy over to hit on me.

They think they're funny.

They're going to find out today that I am not amused.

Okay, that's not technically true. The new guy, while young and cocksure, is very attractive and in any other situation, exactly the kind of man I would have welcomed hitting on me. His interest gave me a small ego boost, not that I would ever admit that to any of them. As one of only a few females in my MOS, I cannot and will not be reduced to my sex in the eyes of my peers or subordinates.

Fuck no.

My vibrator and I have this conversation regularly. I'd rather be celibate than disrespected.

But a different time, a different place, and Saint is the kind of guy I would take home and ride into the morning light.

Kemp pokes his head into the office. "Formation in ten?"

"Yep," I say without looking up from my computer.

"Are you going to flog me and Vale today?" he says with a wry grin. The three of us went through AIT together and have known each other for four years. They are like brothers, so it makes sense I want to hold their heads under water from time to time.

"I'm still deciding."

He chuckles. "I can't wait to see the look on Saint's face when he meets you."

"You are a sick and twisted man, Kemp."

"I really am." He smacks his hand on the doorframe and walks out, leaving me shaking my head.

Tension weaves its way through my shoulders as I contemplate the next two weeks. This is my chance to show the command I'm ready to lead the next deployment coming up in six weeks. There are two teams deploying to separate locales, four K9s per location, two K9 leads.

I want one of those spots.

My anxiety must be palpable because Gwar stands up, stretches, and rests her head in my lap.

"You ready to go show them who's boss?" I rub her head, using my thumbs to trace around her eyes, which she loves.

"Errfff," she half barks, half snorts her agreement.

"Let's do this."

Walking out into the brisk February morning, I survey the dozen K9 handlers with their dogs and the forty support personnel who line up with us. I don't know why they don't have their own formation, but I think it's because the captain hates mornings.

Obviously, the badasses do their own thing.

Sergeant Vale and Sergeant Kemp stand at parade rest with their dogs by their sides facing the formation with more than enough space for me to take center stage. I swear, I can see Kemp's lips twitching as I approach.

I can't help it, my eyes go right to Santiago who Vale put on the end in the front row.

His eyes widen, but to his credit, he keeps his composure.

"For the next two weeks, I will be in charge of the K9 unit in Sergeant First Class Theoroux's absence. As usual, if you have questions, you go to your team leads and then me." Gwar and I walk the line, and I purposefully start with Saint.

No weakness.

"We have a new member joining us today. Most of you know Hades, who is back in commission with a new handler, Private First Class Santiago. I hope you treat the decorated war hero with as much love and respect as her last handler did." I wait for him to break rank and protocol, but to his credit he locks eyes with me and nods.

"Yes, Sergeant LaVey. Hades and I are going to be lifelong friends."

I nod. "Good."

Formation takes less than ten minutes, and then the support personnel break off for PT while the handlers return to the kennels to prep for a day of training.

Gwar and I are walking back to the office when I hear him running up behind me.

"Sergeant LaVey?"

I turn to catch Saint and Hades approach while Kemp and Vale watch from a distance.

"Yes, Private?" I arch my brow and keep the smile off my face. I don't know who else is watching, and I refuse to let anyone think there is anything between us to include the man standing in front of me.

"I wanted to apologize for last night. Like I said, I knew they were setting me up."

"They set both of us up, but don't worry, they'll get theirs today."

He grins and quickly covers it by bowing his head. "You said the next time I saw you, if I still wanted your number, I should ask."

I open my mouth to stop him.

Shaking his head, he glances at the ground. "I'm not going to ask, even though I do still want it. I have to imagine being the only woman on the field this morning was hard, so I'm not going to make it harder by pursuing you... for now."

"For now?"

"I won't always be a Private First Class, and I won't always be under your command. Someday, you and I will meet when the stars align, and then we'll pursue what's between us."

"There is nothing between us, Private Santiago."

"Not yet, ma'am."

Narrowing my eyes, I lower my voice into a near hiss. "As the newest and lowest ranking individual here, you are on kennel duty for the next month. Inform Sergeant Vale that he needs to demonstrate your new duties explicitly, and I'll be there shortly."

"Yes, ma'am." He clicks his tongue, and he and Hades take off at a run toward the kennels.

Shaking my head, I roll my eyes and walk back into the office, already making a mental date with my vibrator for tonight.

Jesus—he's going to be my greatest temptation to date.

"**K**emp, you're in the bite suit." I flash him a smile when he gives me a *you-got-to-be-kidding-me* look.

"Private Santiago, it's time to show us how well you and Hades work together."

Vale and I stand on the sidelines evaluating Santiago, already fully aware that Hades is a world-class military working dog. Her old handler separated six months ago, but Hades is too young to be retired and has at least another three years left in service. Even though she's beautifully trained, not all dogs and handlers get along.

I guess the bitch is as charmed by the cocky eighteen-year-old as I am.

Damn, why'd he have to be young and under my limited command?

Gwar whines, desperate to play considering Kemp is her favorite chew toy. After running through a couple drills and a half-dozen recalls, I tell Santiago and Hades to stand by and then quietly tell Gwar to attack. "Fass."

Kemp turns in time to catch her as she takes him to the ground, using her full body weight and a leap not normally sanctioned in the field. Both Vale and I laugh as Kemp yells in the distance, wrestling on the ground with my dog.

I wait until he yields before calling her off him, jogging up to get within speaking distance, but not close enough that he can swipe my legs out from underneath me. Not that he would while our dogs are in play. "Aus."

"What the hell, LaVey?" He looks up from the ground at me.

I stand over his head with my hands on my hips. "That's what you get for the shit you pulled last night, Kemp."

He chuckles. "It was worth it."

Captain Leiter walks over to Vale and waves me over. He, like most soldiers, knows better than to walk onto the field while the dogs are working.

I jog over with Gwar at my side. "Sir?"

"That was crazy. I don't know how you guys let a dog take you down like that." Captain Leiter shivers.

Vale and I shrug. "All in a day's work. What can we do for you, sir?"

"Deployment list came out. You and Vale will lead the two teams—one in Bagram, the other in Kandahar. I leave it to you to assemble your personnel. Four canines per location. You start training with the rest of your teams next week. If you have questions, I'll be in my office."

"Yes, sir." I tamp down my desire to jump up and down and shriek my excitement.

Vale grins and elbows me playfully. "Hot damn."

"Right?" I glance over my shoulder. "Now who is going to take Kemp with them?"

Vale laughs. "I'll take the FNG if you take Kemp."

Deep down I'm disappointed, but I know if I want to keep my boss babe military bearing, as well as keep my panties on like a good soldier, I need to be as far away from Private Santiago as possible. "Deal."

For the next six weeks, we are training, packing, inventorying, and then getting a week of downtime before leaving the country for an eight-month tour. I've barely seen Vale or Santiago in that time, and probably won't until we come back home next year.

Before I know it, another five months have passed.

Kemp and I are thick as thieves while in garrison. He protects my back—I know this—which makes me feel safe as the only female forward deployed with this team. And he never once lauds it over my head. The guys seem to respect me, or at least they aren't hitting on me, and considering most of them are badass motherfuckers, I'm sure if they didn't respect me things would be a lot worse.

Still, I can't wait until we get home so I can go out to a bar in the one flirty dress I own with makeup on and my hair done. One night, maybe a weekend, is all I need. I can imagine it now, flirting with some hot stranger under the neon lights just to scratch this itch I've had for months. Honestly, I'm already researching singles resorts and thinking about taking a vacation away from anyone who knows me as Sergeant LaVey.

How sad is it that the last man to make me feel like an attractive woman was Saint?

How pathetic is it that all my fantasies are a little too focused on him?

The one man I can't have. Ever.

"Hey." Kemp strolls up to me and my team coming back from patrol.

"Hey back," I reply as Gwar jumps down from the humvee.

"Why don't you give me Gwar and you go pack a bag."

"What are you talking about?" I shake my head as we break off from the rest of the team toward the makeshift kennels, our connexes attached to the back. Yes, we literally sleep with the dogs, but our accommodations are better than the rest of the units.

"There's a flight heading out tonight for Qatar. Seventy-two hours R&R, starting at eighteen-hundred."

"I can't go."

"Yes, Janey, you can. You're the only one who hasn't gone yet, and you deserve a break. Trust me, the time at the pool alone is worth the flight. I've got Gwar and have already cleared it with the commander."

The R&R site in Qatar is rumored to have a decent chow hall, a rec center that serves real beer, a DJ and a dance floor, and as Kemp points out, an outdoor pool with lounge chairs. They even have barbers, hairdressers, masseuse, and nail techs on site. Many of the guys—big, badass soldiers—have gotten their first pedicures while on R&R.

I glance down at my tattered cuticles. "Are you sure?"

"Go, Janey. Get your ass out of here. There isn't another flight scheduled for at least two weeks and things have been quiet lately. It's the perfect time for a break."

Handing him Gwar's lead, I bend down and kiss my princess on the snout before jumping up and placing a chaste kiss against his cheek. "Thanks!"

VETERAN
K9
TEAM

REPORTING
FOR DUTY

Chapter 3
Prologue Continued - Saint

Sitting at a computer in the common area wearing board shorts and flip-flops feels sinfully good. Not better-than-sex good, but it's a close second considering I won't be having any of that for at least another three months. I'm so tired of fucking my hand, especially when I know there are a dozen of us in the shower at any given moment—each man trying his damnedest not to let the guy in the stall next to him know what he is doing.

I mean, we all know what we are doing, but still.

Groaning, grunting, and growling from a good release —who knew I would miss such a simple thing?

My little sister, Demon, sent me an email last night filled with venom, as is her fifteen-year-old way. She has no concept of life outside of our tiny, dying town, and has transferred all of her hate for the world onto me.

That's okay though. I'm her big brother and that's what I'm here for. Once she's old enough—after she graduates high school or turns eighteen, whichever comes first

—I will get her out of there. She'll come live with me—wherever I am at the time—and go to college like a young woman should. I sure as fuck know it won't happen if she stays in Rizona.

I'm parsing through my sister's latest tirade when a female walks through the room. I don't know what it is, but every dick in here is attuned to her presence, twenty sets of eyes leaving whatever held their attention two seconds ago to follow her.

Maybe it's the dead quiet that falls over us upon seeing the first flesh and blood female not wearing a hijab in five months that alerts the pack?

Who knows?

The first thing I lock onto are bare legs and a perfect ass in a pair of board shorts similar to my own. She probably bought them at the Exchange hours before or after I bought mine. That's the funny thing about being R&R when you didn't pack for a vacation, you only have one place to buy clothes, so even though we are out of uniform, we are all essentially wearing the same thing.

Then I notice the blond bob and cute button nose as the female scans the room with her sunglasses shielding her eyes.

"Janey?"

She swings her attention my way, her lips parting in surprise. "Saint?"

"Holy shit." I stand up and wave sappily. I swear, I can hear the collective whoosh of breath as every male in here suddenly realizes that she's not only not alone, but not available.

Suckers!

"I hadn't heard you were given a pass too." She approaches my computer terminal.

"Yeah, I've been here for a day. When did you get here?"

"Last night." Her gaze swings over the common room again. Fuck, is she with someone? How badly would that suck to have her here and not be able to capitalize on this time? For the last five months she's been the only fantasy I've fucked my fist to, my fascination bordering on unhealthy. I don't know what it is about her, but I'm obsessed.

"No shit?" I also look around, wondering who she is looking for. "Are you waiting for someone?"

"Uh, some chick I flew in with last night. She said she knew a couple people who would be here, and we'd all go to the pool together today, but I don't see her."

"I'm going to the pool, if you want some company."

She looks me over, or at least I think that's what she's doing behind her dark sunglasses. "How's Hades?"

"She's doing great and training me well." I grin.

That makes her smile. "How long until you're ready?"

"Let me hit save and we can go."

We walk across the compound together, the desert sun above us brutal in its assault. By the time we get to the pool, we're both drenched in sweat. I don't waste a minute, stripping off my shirt and kicking off my flip-flops to dive into the deep end.

Ah! Sweet fucking relief.

I turn toward the chairs we claimed in time to catch Janey surreptitiously glancing around before pulling off her baggy T-shirt to reveal a sports bra underneath. Then she shimmies out of the board shorts to reveal a pair of spandex bottoms that cling to her ass perfectly.

Fuck me. Thank god the water is cool enough to keep me from getting embarrassingly hard.

I have no doubt being a woman here has to be overwhelming. There are easily twenty guys to every female, and that includes the permanent party assigned here.

As a woman, you either love the attention or you hate it.

From everything I know about Sergeant LaVey, she hates it.

"Come on in. The water's perfect." I make a small splash in her direction.

She goes to the shallow end and uses the steps, swimming toward me leisurely, her eyes still shielded by her sunglasses. "It does feel good."

"Didn't want to wear a bikini, huh?" I waggle my brows, making sure I keep my distance. There is a strict no fraternization policy while on R&R, even though every guy who finds a willing female will fuck every minute they can while on post.

"I didn't want to attract any more attention than necessary. If I could blend into the scenery, I would."

"You couldn't blend if you tried, Janey."

She looks at me over the top of her sunglasses and rolls her eyes. "I know, I know. Too much cock and not enough pussy here. Every female is a ten in a place like this."

"No." I shake my head and stretch my arms out on the pool deck, letting the lower half of my body float in the deep water. "You're beautiful no matter how hard you try to hide behind sunglasses and baggy clothing. I told you that the night we met, and I meant every word."

"Did you tell me I was beautiful?" she teases.

"If I didn't say it out loud, I was definitely thinking it."

"Hmmm." She swims a little and then comes back to me. "How's Vale?"

"He's good. How's Kemp?"

"Also good."

Fuck, I want to touch her. Just a gentle caress of her arm, or maybe a possessive slide of my hand over her hip. The simplest of touches would mean more to me right now than a night full of orgasms.

Okay, that's a lie, but I'd take anything at this moment. Any touch to prove she's mine.

"You want to grab dinner tonight?" I arch my brow.

"Dinner for two in the chow hall. Sounds romantic." She chuckles.

"As romantic as we can get while confined to post. Although, I'll also buy you a couple beers at the rec center tonight."

"Oh my god, a proper date." Janey takes her sunglasses off and dunks her head under the water, coming up with a smile.

"I wish," I mutter, my eyes locked on her.

She narrows her eyes. "It wouldn't be a date, Saint. You know this. Please tell me you understand."

Reluctantly, I nod. "I understand, Sarge."

She sighs and puts her sunglasses back on her face before swimming away from me.

I catch the eyes of a couple of guys on the other side of the pool, their gazes fixed on her as she swims laps. Something possessive within me growls its displeasure at the horn dogs leering after her, and I pull myself out of the pool in a tricep dip that flexes some of my strength. Water runs off my newly honed twenty pounds of pure muscle filling out my chest, although flexing in front of these guys is stupid.

Gone is the lanky kid I was six months ago, and yet, in a place like this where there is nothing to do but eat and work out, I'm not that impressive. Hell, even Vale has put on fifteen pounds of muscle, as have a dozen other guys. Apparently, they all bulk up while on deployment and then shed the weight and muscle while stateside. It's common—and supposedly unavoidable—although I hope to keep my new physique.

Yes, I'm feeling myself even more than I was before— my cockiness now matches my confidence.

I turn in time to catch Janey staring in my direction, her lips parted in surprise.

Oh, fuck yeah.

She wants me too, no matter how hard she fights the temptation.

I can work with this.

She will be mine.

If not here, then when we get back home.

Operation Seduce Janey LaVey is a go.

We hang out at the pool all day. A few guys come over to chat us up, asking where we're deployed and where we call home. I know they are really sizing up our connection, looking for their opportunity to worm their little worms into her pants.

Janey shuts them down with mostly one-word answers, letting me do most of the talking. Deep down I know it kills her to defer to me, especially considering I'm her subordinate, not that these guys know that.

My stomach grumbles, and I hear hers gurgling next to me as if to answer my cry. "You want to grab dinner?"

"Yeah, but I think I'll take a shower first."

"Yeah, me too. Which bay are you in? I'll swing by and pick you up and we can walk to the dining facility together."

Janey slides her board shorts over her bottoms. "I'm in Building Three."

"Me too." I think all the R&R people are in the same building, which is no more than a giant airplane hangar with plywood partitions and bunk beds. I have more privacy back in Afghanistan—sharing a connex with Vale, Scout, and Hades—than I do here, but I'm not complaining.

"Let's meet in the little reading area they have up front. The one right inside the building."

I nod. "Sounds good."

We give ourselves thirty minutes to shower and then meet at the reading nook as scheduled. Janey is wearing a pair of loose fitting linen capris that almost have a skirt flair to them and a deep cut blouse with a tank top underneath. Nothing about her outfit is overtly sexy, and yet my cock jumps all the same.

"You look beautiful," I say softly so as to not have my voice carry through the metal building. The acoustics in this place are psychotic, which means sex sounds are amplified tenfold. Another reason for the no fraternization policy.

She blushes slightly. "Thanks."

"Let's go." I hold the door open for her and walk by her side to the dining facility. It's still hot as hell, but at least the sun is no longer crushing down on us with brutal intent. Tonight the dining facility is throwing a Mongolian BBQ, which is a five-star feast compared to what we've been eating lately, and honestly the food on post isn't all that bad. Both Janey and I grab our plates, my appetite more than doubling over the last six months, and take over the end of a table in the corner of the room.

"Do you want anything other than water to drink?" I tilt my head at her tray, standing up to grab myself a couple glasses of whole milk.

"I'm good, thanks."

Once we're comfortably seated, I launch into Operation Seduce Janey LaVey. "So, Janey, tell me about yourself."

She arches her brow and stares me down over her forkful of noodles. "What do you want to know?"

"Where are you from?"

"Nowhere Colorado. You?"

"Nowhere Texas."

She smiles. "I bet my nowhere is prettier than your nowhere."

"For sure. I'm from a dust pile that was swept off I-10 and forgotten." I down one of my small glasses of water. "Why'd you join the military?"

She shrugs. "I needed a way out of there. You know?"

"I do. I practically enlisted when I was fourteen, meeting with the recruiter and signing a letter of intent upon my graduation. It wasn't legally binding, of course, but I had my sights set on leaving before I started high school."

"You left a sister behind, right?"

I grin, happy she remembered anything I said about myself that night. "Demon, yeah. She's fifteen now and super angry about life. Our mom died a few weeks before I graduated high school, but by then my enlistment date was set. I'd already sworn in and everything, and there was no way in hell I was going to stay behind. She hates me right now, but I'll win her over, eventually."

"How are you going to do that?" Janey asks, truly interested.

"By getting her out of there and giving her a better life. I'm waiting until she's eighteen and has graduated high school, but then I'll bring her to wherever I am. If we enroll her in school, I think I can sign her on to my medical benefits, and that way she'll be covered for a few years until she has her life figured out."

"You're a good big brother."

"She doesn't see it that way right now, but again, I'll win her over, eventually."

"There's that unyielding confidence again." She chuckles and ducks her head ever so slightly, as if she doesn't want anyone else to see her enjoying herself.

That's okay though, because I know this has nothing to do with me and everything to do with being a female in the military. Not just the military, but in a male-domi-nated career field. She doesn't want to be perceived as feminine, or girly, or weak—and I get it.

Truthfully, I don't want her to be anyone other than who she is—a badass K9 handler who happens to be sexy as fuck. If we weren't here, if we weren't military, or if I wasn't roughly her subordinate, maybe she would be both with me. A badass boss babe / K9 handler and sexy temptress all rolled into one. I know I could handle it.

I'd bathe and bask in it daily.

I'd really like to start right now.

"Want to grab a drink after this?"

VETERAN
K9
TEAM
REPORTING
FOR DUTY

Chapter 4
Prologue Continued - Janey

I'd love to tell Saint yes, but going to the rec center for a beer is like being the chum thrown into shark-infested waters. Even with him by my side, all eyes will be on me. While I miss being seen as a sexy woman, the guys here don't see me that way—not really. What they see isn't me, but a female with a hole to be filled through their testosterone-induced lusty haze. Most of these guys wouldn't be interested in me if we were back home where the male-to-female ratio is closer to fifty-fifty.

Saint is honestly the only man here that I know wants me for me. He let me know within minutes of meeting and has never once wavered in his desire. That's going to make my nights alone with my fantasies much more vivid when I get back in a few days.

Thank god I have my own sleeping quarters.

"I don't think so." I shake my head.

"Why not? Because of all these ass-clowns?" He pushes his tray against mine and taps his fork against my glass, bringing my eyes up to his. "You'll be with me. We can't do anything about them looking at you—you're hot and being looked at is unfortunately the price you pay for being beautiful—but I guarantee none of them will touch you when I'm by your side."

He called me beautiful.

Oh Janey. Really?

"I'm not afraid of these guys, but it's a lot to be stared at. You know?"

He nods, his lips twitching as he holds back a big smile. "Yeah, I'm used to women climbing all over me because of how devastatingly handsome I am, but I've gotten used to it. You should too. It's the burden we must bear for being gorgeous."

I roll my eyes. "You and your ego."

Saint chuckles. "Come on, Janey. No one here knows us. We're in civilian clothes. No rank, no last names. Just two people trying to relax with their three-beer limit. We'll listen to music, maybe play some cards, and get to know each other better."

"Okay," I relent.

"Yeah?"

"Yeah."

We enter the rec center, grab a couple of beers and a table on the edge of the dance floor. Saint sits with his back to the wall, his eyes on the crowd to watch my back. Part of me wants to sit next to him so I too can watch our backs, but then we'd be cuddled up and I'm not so sure about that.

"What's the plan when we get back to the states?" Saint asks over his beer.

"What do you mean?"

"I mean, are you a lifer? If so, how long have you been with Ranger Battalion? Do you hope to do all twenty with them, or do you have other plans?"

My jaw drops slightly. "Uh, I think I will do twenty years. I mean, the retirement is too good to pass up. But will it all be Ranger Battalion? I don't know. My long-term goal is to get back to Colorado and open up an animal shelter or training facility or something. I've been thinking a lot about creating a military-focused animal shelter for deploying members to have a safe space to kennel their dogs long term."

"That would be great." Saint leans forward, resting his arms on the table. "A lot of the guys have bitched about missing their dogs while deployed. Some of them don't even know where they are right now because their girlfriends or wives broke up with them while they can't do shit about it."

"Exactly. Deploying is hard enough, and too many animals are surrendered because the service members don't have family or close friends they can trust with their fur-babies."

"Why Colorado? Why not Georgia or North Carolina?"

I shrug. "I want to go home. Colorado is beautiful and Spring City has multiple military installations to cater to. Plus, if I ever start a family, that's where I'd like to be."

"Sounds like you have it all figured out, Janey." Saint

leans back and takes another long draw off his beer. I have to admit, it tastes good after going without for five months. Before I know it, we're both at the bottoms of our mugs. "Want another one?"

"Okay." I slide my glass to him.

"Be right back."

A couple minutes later, he's sliding another beer in front of me and retaking his seat. The DJ plays another round of music, this time louder as a group of guys and a couple chicks—one of whom being the female I flew here with last night—jump on the dance floor.

Saint says something, but I can barely hear him over the music because one of the large speakers is right next to our table.

"What?" I shout back.

He shakes his head, crooks one finger in my direction, and pats the space next to him on the bench.

Dammit.

I grab my beer and slide into the seat next to him. He throws his arm over the top of the bench, behind my shoulders, but doesn't make a move to touch me. I'm not sure how I feel about that. Part of me would like him to pull me close, and then again, it's a horrible idea.

Saint leans into my ear. "I asked you what kind of music you like? You never told me the day we met."

"I did. I told you I like all kinds of music."

"Yeah, but you never told me which song you'd dance with me to."

I shake my head and laugh. "You are never going to give this up, are you?"

His smile fades and his dark eyes peer deep into my soul. "No, I'm not."

Our lips are so close right now that it would take nothing to sink deep into a mind-numbing kiss. The corner of his lips curl when my eyes go down to them, and his eyes sparkle with knowledge he shouldn't have.

Dammit, I want him, and he knows it.

"Someday, Janey, you are going to dance with me." I turn my face from him, looking out at the crowd like one of a dozen spectators, trying to pretend like I'm not falling into his web. His breath tickles the loose hairs framing my face as he continues to speak in a dark, seductive tone. "It'll be slow, our bodies swaying, your softness and my hardness perfectly aligned."

"It's impossible," I mutter more to myself than him.

He continues, completely ignoring any roadblocks I set up for us. "When we dance, it will be Saint and Janey. Janey and Saint. No rank. No rules. Nobody's business but ours and ours alone. It will be our secret until the day it no longer has to be a secret."

VETERAN
K9
TEAM

REPORTING
FOR DUTY

Chapter 5
Saint - Prologue Continued

Fucking hell, this is sweet torture. Having her so close, and yet still unable to touch her, kiss her, taste her like I desire. I want nothing more than to suck her plump bottom lip into my mouth, and I can honestly say that is not something I've ever fantasized about doing with anyone.

We sit in relative silence, watching the small crowd dance, and drink our beers. I'm about to ask her if she'd like another one when she turns to me suddenly. "I'd like to go back to my room now."

Disappointed, I glance at my watch. It's not even twenty-one hundred hours. "Okay."

We toss back the last of our beers—it's not something you waste when you are only allotted three—and walk out of the building side by side. I feel the eyes on us, every man here weighing and measuring me, judging my worth, coveting what appears to be mine.

Suckers.

We enter Building Three and I motion to the rows of plywood rooms, whispering low to keep my voice from carrying in the metal dome. "Which row are you down?"

"Actually, I'm in a connex at the end of this row." She whispers back.

My jaw drops. "You got your own room? How'd you swing that?"

She shrugs. "I guess there weren't enough women to throw us in a bunk room. Do you want to see it?"

I stare into her beautiful blue-green eyes, wondering if I'm misinterpreting her seemingly simple question. She knows damn well I know what the inside of a connex looks like. They are all the same whether here or in Afghanistan.

Is she inviting me into her room?

Her bed?

Doesn't matter, because the only answer I have is yes.

I nod and we wordlessly walk down the aisle, thankfully not passing a single soldier on our trek across the building. She unlocks the door and enters. I follow and close it softly as a light flickers on. Two wall lockers, two twin beds, one A/C unit, and one small table with two chairs. Yep, just like our connexes in Afghanistan.

I stand in place, my eyes locked on her, and keep my voice low. Even though we are in a room, I don't want to risk anyone hearing a man's voice in what I assume is the female quadrant of the living space. "Where's your roommate?"

The bed farthest from the door has personal bedding —not Army issue—which means someone who is permanent party stays here.

Janey waves a piece of paper. "Apparently she spends most of her nights with her boyfriend off post in the contractor village. She told me to have fun while on break."

"Fun?"

She stares back at me before gathering up the hem of her shirt and pulling it over her head. She has on a plain white cotton bra, yet it's the sexiest fucking thing I've ever seen.

I clench my hands at my sides, desperate to reach out for her. But she has to be first to touch me, has to initiate what I want most in the whole wide fucking world. Taking a few tentative steps toward me, she slides the tips of her fingers into my waistband and pulls me forward so that our chests touch. "This never happened."

"Roger that." I lean my head down, my lips hovering above hers.

She raises up on her toes and presses her mouth against mine, and that's all the permission I need. I wrap my arms around her small, muscular body and fill my hands with her lush ass, pulling her tightly against me. I'm not tall compared to my brethren, just barely over six foot, but Janey climbs me like a tree all the same. Pressing her back against the cool metal wall, she lets out a gasp while clawing at my shirt.

I pin her in place with my hips and lean back to give

her room to pull my shirt over my head, our mouths separating long enough to put us skin to skin. Then I'm plunging my tongue back into her plush mouth, swallowing her soft moans and heady whimpers.

Fuck this woman is all I've wanted for months, and part of me fears I'm dreaming right now and this is nothing more than another wet dream. If so, I hope I don't call out her name or dump a load of cum on my sheets while Vale watches over me.

He'd never let me live that down.

Janey gasps for air, tilting her head back and giving me access to her neck, her chest, her breasts. "You've gotten big during this deployment."

"Pure muscle, baby—all for you."

"Lay me down, Saint. I want to feel you on top of me."

Fuck me. Don't have to ask me twice. "Say less."

I turn in the small space and set one knee down on the twin-size bed, lying her flat on her back. Gazing down at her, I smile as I run my hands over her breasts and her flat stomach to the waistband of her pants. "You are so fucking beautiful."

"I'm glad you think so." She shimmies her hips, as I pull them off her, her panties basic white cotton to match her bra.

Again—simply stunning.

Janey reaches for my pants and I stop her, shaking my head slowly. "You're not in charge here, LaVey. I've been dreaming about tasting you for six months, and now that I have you underneath me, I'm going to take my time and savor it." I pull her leg up and rest her ankle on my shoulder, turning my face and kissing her calf. She watches me intently, her breathing shallow as I move my way up the inside of her thigh with my tongue. Cupping her pussy over her cotton barrier, I moan softly at the wet heat pressing against my fingertips.

She wants me, but I have to make sure after tonight, she can't live without me.

I hook my fingers into the waistband and slide her panties down her legs, setting her feet flat on the bed and pushing her knees apart with my broad shoulders. "I know we can't be loud, so if you have to scream into a pillow, be my guest. But I want your hands on me, Janey. I want you to let me know what you like and what you love, so I can do it again and again and again."

"Cocky," she whispers.

I grin. "Confident."

Lowering my head, it takes one swipe of my tongue to know I'm hooked and there will never be a drug that makes me as high as the taste of Janey on my lips. I bury my face in between her legs, licking and sucking until she's bucking her hips and riding my mouth with one hand in my hair, the other covering her lips as she fights to stifle her cries of ecstasy. Although I'd prefer to hear her cursing the gods in my name, her muffled cries when I slide two fingers inside her has my dick painfully hard and pressed against the zipper of my jeans.

Janey's legs shake uncontrollably. Her cunt clamps down and an orgasm crashes over as I slow down my assault on her clit and press firm kisses to her thighs. "You are fucking delicious."

"And you are talented." She unhooks her bra by flicking the clasp in the front, baring herself to me. I sit up and unlace my boots, kicking them off before standing and unbuttoning my jeans. Janey watches with rapt fascination as if I were doing a striptease. Part of me wants to put on a show by pushing my jeans and boxers down in one fluid movement, the other part doesn't want to be out of touching distance any longer than necessary.

Completely naked, I stroke my hard length and look down at her. "I don't have a condom, but we both had complete physicals before we came."

She nods. "I'm not worried about disease, but I have one thing to ask."

"What's that, baby?" I kneel between her splayed thighs and lower myself to my elbows, trailing kisses up her stomach to her breasts.

"Even though I'm on the pill, I think you should pull out, just in case."

Something primal within me roars because the image of her swollen with my child feels natural, and yet she's absolutely right. Now is not the time.

I nod and bring my eyes up to hers. "Of course."

I kiss her softly at first with my cock nestled against her hot, wet heat, wanting to sear this moment into my brain for later. I have to remember every taste, every smell, every sound. Each nerve ending needs to memorize what it felt like the first time I slipped inside her welcoming body. That memory will be what fuels my fantasies until the next time I get to touch her.

Janey slides her hands up my biceps and then down my back, crossing her ankles behind my hips as she lifts her ass to silently beg me to push forward. Our kiss turns fevered and I'm once again swallowing her moans, the head of my cock slipping into the perfect spot where it takes very little to push forward and sink slowly into her tight channel.

A groan pushes past my lips as her heat envelopes me. "Fuck. Your pussy feels amazing. Everything about you is perfect."

"Oh, Saint. Shut up and fuck me."

Chuckling, I smile down at her sassiness. "I'm going to fuck you, Janey, but I'm also going to take my time and treasure everything little thing there is to learn about you."

As if to prove my point, I draw myself back slowly, savoring every fraction of an inch sliding against her g-spot. Janey has her eyes closed, her head back, mouth agape, as if she too is luxuriating in every nerve ending firing pulses of pleasure into her brain.

Part of me wants to drag this out as long as possible, but with each push and pull of my hips—the ecstasy crossing her face and the dopamine flooding my brain— it's not long before I'm losing control and rushing toward my own orgasm. I slam my hips forward hard, and a gasp escapes Janey's lips as her inner walls tighten around me.

Oh, she likes it hard and rough.

Okay, then. I can do that too, even though it means I

will blow my load a lot earlier than I'd like. If I was coming inside her, I could push through and keep fucking until I was hard again—it's one of my superpowers—but pulling out will probably fuck up that rhythm.

That's okay though. I just need to make her come again.

I alternate slamming my hips forward and pumping through a few slow short strokes until Janey's digging her fingers into my biceps and moaning a little louder than appropriate given our tight, acoustic quarters. "Yes. Right there, Saint. Don't stop. Please don't stop."

Pressing my mouth down on hers, I swallow her moans and murmur against her lips. "I'll never stop giving you what you need, Janey."

She comes apart, her pussy spasming around my cock, causing my balls to tighten up and cum to race up my shaft. I pull out as I release, spewing my load all over her lower stomach. Clenching my jaw, I press my forehead against her chest and growl as my cock continues to pulse and jump between our bodies.

Fuck that was intense.

Both of us pant to catch our breath. Janey slides her hands softly up my back, lovingly rubbing small circles over my shoulder blades until both of our pulses have slowed back to normal. "There's a washcloth on the hook inside my wall locker."

I nod, pull back to look her in the eye, kiss her on the lips, and then lift to sit on my heels. The wall locker is six inches from the bottom of the twin bed, so it takes nothing to open the door, grab the washcloth, and clean her and then myself. I don't even have to climb off the bed.

Stretching out next to her, I pull her to her side and brush her short blonde hair back from her face. Using my fingers, I softly trace every inch of her, following the smooth curve of her jaw, the soft length of her neck, the gentle slope of her breast until her nipple hardens from my touch.

Fuck, I could spend hours exploring her.

She does the same, tracing the curves of my pecs and the division of abdominal muscles in my stomach. Chuckling softly, she murmurs, "You're still hard."

"Oh yeah. I can go all night, again and again."

Janey brings her blue-green eyes up to mine. "Really?"

I grin. "I'll go until you beg me to stop."

She raises her brow. "I don't beg."

"Well, then, I guess we're only stopping for water and bathroom breaks. I can eat when I get back to garrison tomorrow night."

Giggling, she shakes her head, and then a mask of seriousness takes over. Her words are barely above a whisper as she pins me with eyes filled with dread. "Don't make me regret taking you to my bed, Saint."

I shake my head. "I won't, Janey. Until you're ready, this is our secret. But understand, I don't want just one night with you. If that's all you can offer right now, I'll take it, but what I want will take a lifetime to satiate. Understand?"

"You are very intense for a man your age, you know that?"

"This has nothing to do with age and everything to do with deep-seated, innate knowledge that you and I could have something special—damn the *right time, right place* nonsense. Someday, the stars will align for us. I'm confident."

VETERAN
K9
TEAM
REPORTING
FOR DUTY

Chapter 6
Janey

Present Day

"You'll be at Karden's house for Saint's DD214 BBQ, right?" Kemp pokes his head in my door.

"Of course." I force a smile as I say the words, trying to hide the trepidation building in my belly.

Kemp looks across the bay and then walks in and closes my door behind him.

Well, shit. This can't be good.

He sits in my guest chair, his knees spread wide, elbows resting on his thighs, fingers steepled under his thick beard. Considering the size of his biceps, he looks uncomfortable.

"Yes?" I say casually, although I'd bet Vegas money I know what this is about.

"What are we going to do about you two?"

"Us two? Who is *us two*?" Oh yeah, I'm one hundred

percent going to play the clueless card right now because this is a conversation I do not want to have.

"Come on, Janey, don't play dumb. It doesn't suit you." Kemp leans back in his chair. "You recruited him, so you must've realized that you were going to have to deal with him."

"What? I am dealing with him."

"In the last week he's been here, you have been out of the office seventy-five percent of the time, and the rest of the time you've locked yourself in this office while you make me and Vale run him through all the operational norms."

"On-the-job training..." I shrug. "What's the problem?"

Kemp shakes his head. "I know you better than anyone, LaVey, and even though you've never admitted it, I know something happened between you. I'm betting the first time was on R&R in Qat—"

"You couldn't possibly know that," I interrupt.

He quirks his brow, and his massive reddish brown beard hides any tilt of his lips. "Well... both of you went on R&R at the same time, and neither of you mentioned seeing each other while you were there. We've all been to Qatar, Janey, and it's not big enough for the two of you to not have run into each other. Your silence was very telling."

Narrowing my eyes, I say nothing while shaking my head. Can't deny it, but I will go to my grave not confirming it. If he knows about that time, how many other times does he know about?

"If you aren't going to work with him, why bring him on?" Kemp continues.

I sigh and put my pen down. "Like we couldn't invite him in? He belongs here just as much, if not more than Linc or Karden. He's been with us since the beginning. It was me, you, Vale, Barron, and then Saint."

"You'll get no argument from me. He belongs here, but if the two of you can't get along—" Kemp licks his lips and shakes his head again. "It's disrupting the harmony of the office, Janey. Everyone can feel the tension between you two, so if there is shit to hash out, you better do it... soon."

I'm working hard not to clench my jaw or shoot lasers through my eyeballs at the messenger, but it's difficult. Still, I have nothing I can say to him.

Or more to the point, nothing I should say.

Kemp puts on his big brother tone—soft, nurturing, but also kind of a smartass. It's the one he used when he found out about Hugo and came to me in the hospital. No way I would've ever called him—or anyone else for that matter—but he came for me anyway and barged his way into my business. "What can I do to help you?"

Shaking my head, I cast my eyes down to my hands that are in my lap. My cuticles are chewed up again—a bad habit I picked up at some point to handle my stress. I hadn't realized I've been chewing on them until now.

Well shit.

"He hates me," I say barely above a whisper, my eyes glued to the paperwork on my desk.

"If he does, he hasn't said shit to us. You know none of us would allow that to slide."

I close my eyes and take a deep breath. It doesn't matter if he hates me because this is my burden to bear and shouldn't affect the office or my green-blooded family. "Fine. I'll have a talk with him, but not at his party. Sometime next week."

Kemp raps his knuckles against my desk and stands. "Okay. What are you bringing tomorrow?"

"What do you think?" I roll my eyes.

"Lemon bars." He grins as he opens my door. "Otherwise, you'll have fifteen hundred pounds of testosterone and muscle whining because you've denied us our favorite treat."

"Fifteen hundred pounds? I don't think you're giving your gym routines enough credit. I'm betting you're short three hundred pounds between the eight of you." I work with beasts. Each one of them are muscle-bound knuckleheads.

To be fair, I'm only slightly better. I've always been more successful at building muscle than achieving an hourglass figure. Cher and Mari are perfectly proportioned—lots of tits and ass—which is every man's fantasy.

Me? I've always been built like a boy. A four-wheeling, mudslinging, tree-climbing tomboy from day one.

Cher and Mari are also tomboys, but they're curvy ones. Yeah, I might be a little jealous.

"See you tomorrow." Kemp smacks my door frame and then calls Krieger to him. A few minutes later the front door opens and closes, the silence from beyond my office deafening in the team's absence.

I glance at the security cameras, noting with a small sense of relief that the parking lot is empty minus my Dodge Charger.

Macha, my three-year-old Rottweiler, comes up and pushes her muzzle into my lap. "Time to run home, girl?"

I've been spending a lot of nights out here now that we have puppies. Since I'm the only one who doesn't have someone to go home to, I've done what I can to make my travel trailer homier. Logan offered to buy and build a three-bedroom doublewide on the property, but I told him no.

Part of me wishes I had said yes, but he's too generous with his money, and the last thing I want is for him to feel used.

But as we get more puppies, one of us will have to live out here on the property, and considering it is legally mine, it might as well be me. Maybe I'll talk to Logan about financing me in the interim, so I can sell my house in town and move out here permanently.

Fuck—yeah, I guess that's what I'll have to do.

Macha and I do one more pass through the kennels—checking on the puppies in their playpen and the two dogs we are kenneling while their owners are away at military schools—before sliding into my car and heading back to town. It takes a couple of hours to do laundry, eat dinner, bake three dozen lemon bars, shower, and pack up for another night out at the center.

By the time Macha and I are settled in the travel

trailer, it's nearly ten at night. I know the puppies would be fine by themselves throughout the night—they are five months old now and have everything they need in their pen—but I hate not being within earshot.

As I settle in the bed, the script I need to hash out before I see and talk to Saint replays in my head.

Part of me thinks I should approach it casually.

Like legit, sit him down and say, *"Hey bro, are we cool? I mean, I know you've explored every part of my body and made me come in ways I didn't even know I could come, and there was that time you said you loved me, but that was years ago, so let's pretend like none of that ever happened and be coworkers and business partners and I'll just sit by quietly while you meet some other woman and fall in love and make her the happiest woman ever. So we're cool, right?"*

Yeah, I bet that will go over really well with him. I'm not surprised he hasn't talked shit about me to the guys. He's always been good at hiding his feelings from everyone except me—and only when we're alone. But, considering I went radio silent after he told me he loved and wanted to marry me, there's no way he cannot hate me today.

To add insult to injury, six months later I was pregnant—which is the only reason I married Hugo—but the worst part is I never had the lady-balls to tell Saint myself.

Instead, I let the rumor mill do its job—like the complete chicken shit I am.

Not that it matters. My pregnancy didn't last four

months and my marriage didn't last two. Hugo turned out to be an abusive asshole who, during an argument one night, beat the shit out of me and sent me to the hospital. He fled the area, and is now serving ten years in Leavenworth for desertion, aggravated assault, and voluntary manslaughter.

Even if I had wanted to call Saint, I couldn't. Not for that. Not after what I've done to him. I didn't deserve his comfort then, nor his forgiveness now, but he deserves a piece of the VKC pie, so I better come up with the words to make this right.

*E*ighteen hours later, we're eating, drinking, and rehashing old war stories in Karden's big, corner lot backyard. I've known half of these guys for ten years, but in some ways I'm seeing a side of them I've never seen before. Each man now has a woman he can't seem to keep his hands off of, and they're openly displaying a gentle, teasing, loving, and nurturing nature I had no idea they were capable of.

All Kemp has to do is arch his brow at his woman, Mari, and she's melting onto his lap. Vale doesn't let his wife, Cher, lift a finger, making sure she has everything she needs while lovingly looking after her and his infant, Cari. He's such a doting husband and father—which is something I never knew he had in him.

Barron was a codgy old bastard by the time he was twenty-eight, but his much younger woman, Betty, has sparked new life into him. Linc has the kind of devotion to his lady, Brandi, that reminds me of how Saint used to be with me on those rare occasions when we could act like there was something real between us. She grounds his wanderlust daredevil energy, as if in her he finally found home.

Karden might be the one who surprised me the most. Outside of his love for his dog, Kiki, I didn't think he had a nurturing bone in his body. There's a killer instinct to him that always frightened me a little. I know enough about Sylvie from the years of talking with Saint to know she's a spitfire who requires the kind of firm but loving hand Karden apparently has. Who knew?

I don't know Logan or Bishop very well, but I see how they are with their women. Apparently I've been serving with a bunch of fucking marshmallows the last ten years and didn't even know it.

Either that, or it took the right women to turn them into gooey piles of fluff.

I'm standing near a giant bucket of long necks while Saint tells a story from his last deployment that we all can commiserate with. While talking, he stands up and drains the last of his bottle, dumping it in the trashcan near the back door. I grab a beer, pop the top, and hold it out for him as he approaches the bucket. The beer in my hand causes him to stumble over his words as he brings his eyes to mine for the first time in a week.

"Thanks."

"No problem," I say, spinning back to the bucket and grabbing myself one.

God, I forgot about his eyes. His are a rich, chocolate color with specs of green and gold in them. Someone casually looking at him from afar would never see them, but if they stared into his eyes—like I have when he's been on top of me—the beauty is hard to miss.

For the next hour, the sixteen of us sit around and catch up, feeling like a family again—a potentially dysfunctional family, but that's not new for any of us. I notice that Sylvie and Charity spend more and more time in the kitchen, away from the fire pit and our stories. Charity's brother, Chad "Jester" Miller, was killed in action a little over a year ago. A sniper had Bishop, Logan, and Saint pinned down, not that it mattered to Miller because he died instantly. Bishop was his best friend, which is how he met Charity last Christmas. I don't know for sure, but I suspect Miller's death and Saint's involvement in the firefight scared the living hell out of Sylvie, which is why both of them keep disappearing during the war stories.

Vale and Cher stand up and signal the beginning of the end of the night. "The little one is kicking, so I need to get my wife home and in bed."

Saint snorts. "Man, never thought I'd see you fucking whipped."

Half of us look at Saint in surprise while Kemp reaches out to smack the back of his head.

Vale frowns and shakes his head. "It'll happen to you

someday, youngin'. When you meet the right woman, there isn't anything you won't do for her."

The tension that has been circulating the office for the last week immediately thickens upon Vale's words. I look up into the trees, suddenly fascinated with the nonexistent birds not chirping above.

"I'll take your word for it," Saint grumbles while rubbing the back of his head.

Barron, Betty, Linc, and Brandi also stand up, as if they were waiting for somebody to initiate the goodbyes. They clean up their mess and fist bump Saint, "We're going to take off too. Glad you're home, man."

Oh shit. The crowd is thinning quickly and I need to pack up my shit before I'm the last one standing.

I'm waylaid by Charity, who wants to talk about their new Rottweiler puppy—the one we are training to be a PTSD service animal for Bishop—named Jester. Yes, they named her after her fallen brother, and I can't think of a more perfect name considering everything involved. While my Rottweiler, Macha, is not Jester's mom, they are half-sisters, removed by a couple of years.

Charity and Tess have become fast friends, made more clear by the fact that Tess, Logan, and Bishop walk up with plans to do couples things after this.

I've never been the type to have girlfriends, and after spending an afternoon with so many happy couples, I feel even shittier about my life than usual. Karden and Saint walk everybody out, and I use the time to clean up the little mess that remains. Sylvie has been on top of it this evening, not letting one dirty dish sit for more than a few seconds.

Like I said, she seems to keep herself distracted.

With everything cleaned up, I grab my cooler and my empty lemon bar trays, and walk into the kitchen at the same time I hear Karden say, "Maybe you should go to Janey's for a bit."

VETERAN
K9
TEAM
REPORTING
FOR DUTY

Chapter 7
Saint

"Hey, Demon."

"Bro." Sylvie faces the spotless sink with no dishes to focus on.

"You've been hiding in here all night. Do you not like my friends?" I lean against the counter next to her, making it impossible for her to ignore me.

"I like *my* friends just fine. I've been hanging out with them for months."

That makes me smile. At least when we're bickering, we're almost talking. It seems like it's the only way we communicate anymore. "Good. Then why are you hiding?"

"I'm not hiding."

"Yeah, you are. You've been hiding from me since I arrived in town last week."

She rolls her eyes and throws the towel down. "How can I avoid you? You live here."

She tries to walk out on me, but without thinking, I

grab her upper arm and pull her to my chest. "We need to hash this out, Demon."

"Not right now we don't." She tries to yank her arm away, but it only causes me to tighten my grip. Maybe I'm too drunk for this right now. While Sylvie and I have our history, I'm also dealing with a bunch of unresolved shit with Janey, and each day I'm here I'm more on edge.

Jesus. Why the hell did I move to a place where I have two women who barely make eye contact with me? Nine days in Spring City, and Janey has spent less than ten minutes in the same room as me. Tonight is the first time we've looked each other in the eye, and that about killed me.

Seriously... my heart clenched the minute I looked into her beautiful blue-green eyes, freckled nose, and that damn scar marring her left cheek.

"Let her go," Karden barks, which only pisses me off more.

I drag my gaze from Sylvie to my best friend and let go of her arm. "Back off, man. That's my sister."

He pulls Sylvie against his chest and wraps his arm around her waist. "Yeah, but she's my woman."

I stare at them for a minute, a red haze filling my vision. They became *them* a few months ago after I sent him down to Texas to watch over her. He broke the bro code by hooking up with my little sister, but it was the only way to get her out of there—or so I keep telling myself. I wasn't sure they'd make it this long, but as far as I can tell he's good for her, and she gives him something he was missing too.

Fuck me. The smart thing to do would be to walk away, but I'm not feeling very smart right now.

"We need to have a family meeting," I mutter, tipping back my beer bottle and draining the last of its contents.

"Yeah, we do—" Karden agrees "—but not tonight. Maybe you should go to Janey's for a bit."

"What?" Janey pops into the kitchen with her cooler on her shoulder and car keys in her hand.

Karden arches his brow. "Just to hang out for a bit and get Saint out of the house."

Janey glances down at her watch. "I guess it is early. Want to hit the local joint and play a round of pool?"

I can't look at Janey anymore than she can look at me. It hurts too fucking much. I love her. I've loved her since the day I met her. And I've had no problems telling her so.

Unfortunately, she's never said it back.

To this day, I don't know why she married that douchebag. I suppose it was because she got pregnant—but what hurt most was that when it all went down, she never called me. If anyone should've been there for her, it should've been me.

Not Kemp.

Even though I've loved her my entire adult life, ours has been a series of stolen moments and bad timing. We couldn't be together when I was her subordinate, and otherwise we've been stationed at different locations across the country trying our best to live our separate lives. I've dated plenty of women, and I knew she was dating other men, but not even in my worst nightmares did I believe she'd end up with one of them.

I really thought we were passing time until we could be together—no more, no less.

When I found out she was married, my entire world imploded. Of course, I found out while home on leave dealing with my father's funeral arrangements. Add that to fighting with Sylvie about giving up the house, the bar, and moving away to go to school, and that was a really dark time in my life.

I keep my gaze glued to Sylvie during this exchange. She's been mad at me for more than ten years, and nothing I've done has bought me an ounce of forgiveness. I know I fucked up by leaving her at such a young age— especially after our mom died—but there was nothing else I could do. I was fighting for my life, and a bus ticket with a promise of a new beginning was the only thing that kept me from fucking killing myself in high school.

The promise of escape is the only reason I'm alive today.

Still, I know I fucked up, and I have no idea how to get her to forgive me.

I shake my head—disappointed in myself, Sylvie, everything—and nod in Janey's direction. I guess I'll take the lifeline she's offering, even if it is begrudgingly given. "Pool sounds good."

Janey drives because it's obvious I should not be behind the wheel.

"Still haven't won her over, huh?" Janey says while keeping her eyes on the road.

"I don't know what I'm going to do about her."

"Maybe there's nothing for you to do. She's a grown ass woman, Saint, and has been taking care of herself for a long time."

"Actually, she hasn't been taking care of herself." I hiss. "That's why I had to send Karden down there, and now…"

I shake my head. I really don't want to say something I'm going to regret. Instead, I shut my mouth as Janey pulls her Dodge Charger into the Last Stand Saloon's parking lot where Sylvie and Tess usually work on Friday and Saturday nights.

"Does it bother you that Karden and Sylvie hooked up?" Janey asks as we walk across the parking lot, flashing our IDs at a muscle-bound beast named Denny who matches Karden in height and weight.

"No? Yes?" I shrug. "I don't fucking know. If things keep going good, I'm happy for them, but if it goes to shit, it makes it even messier between me and her, and possibly me and Karden."

"You've always been the protective big brother, but I think he's got this one."

"I hope so," I say, leaving it at that.

We grab a pool table and a bucket of beers, taking up residence in a corner of the fairly large country bar. This place has a bit of everything to include a small stage for a house band, a giant circular wood floor perfect for two-stepping, and a mechanical bull run by an ex-rodeo star out back. They also have decent food. Me and the guys have eaten here at least three times since I've been home.

Janey breaks and sinks a couple solids before handing over the cue to me. I line up the shot, but my heart's not in it. Now that I've loosened my tongue and opened the floodgates, my mind is on a roll. "Do you know what she did last week while I was looking at houses?"

"No. What?" Janey sits patiently, as if she also couldn't care less about the game and is fine with letting me rant for a while.

"She handed me her bank account—the one that I set up for her after getting out of AIT." I hand Janey the cue and retake the stool in the corner. "As soon as I could, I set up a checking account and had five hundred dollars per paycheck directly deposited into it. A thousand dollars a month for nine years. It was the money she was supposed to be using to live. I wanted her to leave home after graduation and move to San Antonio, Houston, or fuck, even Austin. Anywhere that wasn't Rizona, Texas. It wasn't enough to live on without having a job, but it should've taken the edge off."

Clenching my jaw, I drain my beer and set down the empty. "I deposited over one hundred thousand dollars, and last week she hands me a bank card with eighty-three thousand in it. She told me to use it as a down payment on my house."

Shaking my head again, I grab a fresh beer out of the bucket. "How am I not supposed to take that as a giant fuck you? Instead of using the money I sent her, she lived well below poverty and scrounged for food. After our father died, she occasionally went without electricity or running water. When I found out, I took those bills over and made sure they were paid."

"Damn. That's—" Janey bites her lip "—one stubborn chick."

I snort. "You got that right."

The more beer that goes down my throat, the looser my tongue gets, and the easier I find it to look Janey in the eye—that is, when she can bring herself to look back.

"No matter how much I love her, or how hard I've tried to take care of her, or how many times I've asked her to let me be there for her, she continuously cuts me out."

Every word coming out of my mouth now has a double meaning. The words I say are aimed at Sylvie, but the underlying subtext is one hundred percent Janey, and she knows it considering she's now standing near me, but staring across the bar that's getting busier by every passing minute.

"But if it comes down to it, Karden will pick her over me. He has to, because as he said, she's his woman. So maybe I lose a sister and my best friend?"

"That's not going to happen." Janey shakes her head, her eyes locked on something or maybe nothing in the distance. "Karden is not going to give either of you up. He might make you fight each other—lock you in a padded room until you work through whatever bullshit you've carried around for so long—but unless you did something unforgivable to her, he's not going to let this tension between you slide for much longer."

"I hope you're right." I down another bottle like its water and grab the last bottle out of the bucket. Janey is still drinking her first, which means I've downed five in the last forty-five minutes. One every ten minutes—even I know that's not good.

Janey chews on her lip, the two of us sitting together in an awkward silence. There are so many things I want to say to her, but considering the last meaningful thing was "I want to marry you"—to which she climbed out of bed shaking her head and saying, "It's amazing what crazy shit a good orgasm can make a guy say"—I don't think there's much left for me to say.

"Are you done with this table?" A group walks up and motions to the forgotten pool game.

"Yeah." I hand them the cue and turn to Janey. "Could you drop me off at a motel?"

"A motel?"

"I don't think I should go back to Karden's tonight. No reason to pour gasoline on the fire right now, you know?"

She nods and sets down her half-drunk beer. "Yeah. You're probably right. Are you ready to go?"

I was raised in a household where you let nothing, especially beer, go to waste. I down my bottle and hers before standing up, the full effect of the alcohol hitting me. "Yeah."

Janey passes two motels before entering a neighborhood a few city blocks from Karden's place. "Where are we going?"

"I have an extra room. No reason for you to pay for a motel."

"You think that's a good idea?" I turn to look at her.

She keeps her eyes forward and sighs. "Probably not, but I hate wasting money."

Macha greets us at the door, and I hear the three puppies yipping in the garage. "You brought them home?"

"I didn't want to drive out to the center after the party."

We enter the garage where three adolescent dogs clamor for our attention. I sit down on the concrete floor at the same time she opens their large kennel door. Instantly I'm mauled by clumsy sharp claws and sharper teeth as they climb all over me. At nearly five months old, I shouldn't be letting them get away with this kind of rough housing while they are in training, but I need this more than they need discipline.

"You're lucky Luce isn't here to see this. You'd be getting an attitude for a week." Janey chuckles.

"Yeah, my girl is a jealous bitch, but I like that about her." I rub my face into one of the fifty-pound puppies' necks.

"I'm going to make up the spare room while you play. Can you take them out to potty? There's a door to the backyard over there." Janey points to another door and leaves me with Macha and the pups.

I haven't spent a lot of time with Macha considering Janey has been avoiding me around the center, but the few times we've put Luce, which is short for Lucifer, and Macha together, they've gotten along really well. Way better than their handlers.

The Rottweiler pushes her big block head into my

chest as I scratch behind her ears, and then she turns around, backs up, and plops her ass down on my thigh—claiming me as her own.

If only it was that easy with humans.

Pushing off the floor, I take the pups outside before getting them resettled in their kennel. Macha and I walk into the house, and I take my first look around Janey's place. She decorates with a southwestern flair, to include a faux leather cowhide rug. I know it's fake—otherwise, Macha would have eaten it by now—but it's the beautiful hand-carved steer's head over her fireplace that reminds me of our Santa Fe weekend. We met at a hot spring resort that had a private mineral water tub inside our cabana. That's when I told her I wanted to marry her.

I wonder if this decor reminds her of that weekend too?

If so, does she think back on it fondly or with regret?

I wander down the hallway until I find her in the spare bathroom next to a room with the light on. Without asking, exhaustion coupled with intoxication takes over and I flop down on the bed, my arms spread wide, my eyes glued to the fan overhead as the ceiling spins slowly.

What should have been is all my brain can handle right now.

"I put fresh towels in the bathroom and there's a brand new toothbrush next to the sink."

"You have spare toothbrushes lying around?"

"I stockpile from my dentist appointments, and I might have a slight problem hoarding tiny shampoo and conditioner bottles from my hotel stays over the years."

"That's right. I remember you stuffing them into your luggage." You can feel the oxygen suck out of the room as soon as the words come out of my mouth.

"Listen, Saint. I'm sorry I've been avoiding you in the office since you got into town. It's just the last time we saw each other—" Her voice trails off.

"Do you really want to talk about that day?" This is better. Not looking each other in the eye for this long overdue conversation is much better.

I have two go-to emotions. I'm either super chill or super pissed. Usually the super pissed only comes out when I'm buzzed but not drunk, which is how I've avoided instigating fights over the years. If I'm drinking, it's not for a buzz, it's to get shitfaced—but I'm a happy drunk.

Only Sylvie knows how to get me angry with a quickness, but she's been perfecting that skill since she was three years old.

Well, her and Janey, but she's never been on the receiving end of my temper, and she never will. I can argue with my sister all day long—snark and sass are part of our love language—but I never have fought with Janey.

Maybe that was our problem? Maybe I should have fought with her more. Verbally, of course, never physically, because until earlier tonight I've never laid my hands on a woman. Damn, I regret grabbing Sylvie's arm. That's not like me, and I'll have to apologize when I see her tomorrow.

"No, but I also don't want things to stay strained

between us. It's affecting the guys, and that's completely my fault." Janey sighs and leans against the doorjamb.

I lift on my elbows and bring my eyes to hers. "I don't want our past affecting the guys in the office either. Maybe I shouldn't have come?"

She vehemently shakes her head. "You belong here with us. The VKC is as much yours as it is mine. We just have to come to a middle ground where we can be friends."

I don't want to be friends, I think. "I can do that."

Smiling, she drops her eyes to the ground. "Sleep good, Saint. I'll see you in the morning."

She walks down the hallway with Macha following behind her and closes the door to her room. Janey LaVey, the only woman I've ever loved, is a mere thirty feet away from me, and yet there might as well be another ocean separating us. While active duty, I grabbed every rotation I could as an escape from my problems back home. Deep down I know this is true, and it almost got me killed.

Now that I'm a civilian, I have to figure out how to let go of the past and live my life. No more running. No more hiding from my problems.

It'd be great if someone could tell me exactly how the fuck to do that.

VETERAN
K9
TEAM
REPORTING
FOR DUTY

Chapter 8
Janey

Things around the office return to normal. I haven't closed my door once this week, and I'm training alongside the other handlers like usual. Of course, I have business calls and paperwork to handle, which means I don't get to play nearly as much as the guys.

But that's part of the job.

Logan walks into my office with a shit-eating grin on his face. "Conference room, ten minutes."

"What?"

He doesn't wait to give me an answer, shouting to the rest of the team the same four-word declarative sentence.

We all file into the conference room and grab coffee or energy drinks from the fully-stocked refrigerator. Since Logan has come on, things around here have gotten a lot nicer. Food for us, yummies for the dogs from Tess's Treats, and new equipment with updated furniture. He says it's an investment into the business, but I think he just wants to take care of us. It's only been three months since he came on, but he has already bought the twenty acres to the west of us, found a general contractor, and had an architect draft county-approved building plans. The first survey crew comes out next week, and the week after that, the land should be cleared for construction.

He and Bishop work out of a hundred thousand-dollar class-A RV which he parks on the other end of the parking lot. The damn thing looks more like a rock band tour bus than an office, but whatever.

Bishop fist bumps Saint, the two of them taking seats next to each other across the room from me and Kemp. Even though we're working towards all of us being equal partners, there is an unspoken division in our ranks. Vale, Barron, Kemp, and I are the old guard. Karden, Linc, Logan, Saint, and Bishop are the youngins'—even though there are only a couple of years separating most of us.

Of course, a couple of years in the Army is the difference between private and NCO, grunt and leadership.

I smile when Saint looks my way, his brow arching slightly. I can't seem to help but know where he is at all times. Even though things between us seem cool to the casual observer, the two of us haven't talked anymore since Saturday night. The next morning we woke up, had a cup of coffee, and I drove him back to Karden's house. I don't even know if he and Sylvie have talked things through yet. Not that he's under any obligation to tell me about what's going on in his life.

Logan attaches his computer to the big screen, another thing he's brought in over the last few months, and brings up promo footage from the *Before Dawn* movie franchise. "As of next week, the Mejer Veteran K9 Stunt Academy will be officially open. Since we don't have our own buildings yet, I want to use the training space to host Brady and his dogs for two weeks while he runs you guys through exercises. Meanwhile, I also want to use the empty building to build an obstacle course for the next film, *After Sunset*. My brothers will come out and train with the dogs for a couple of weeks, which means they'll be bringing security and trailers and all that Hollywood bullshit with them. Obviously with Knox out here, some paparazzi and onlookers will follow, so I wanted to get everyone's agreement and see who is interested in training with Brady for the stunt dogs."

The guys look around. Saint and Linc nod their agreement, but Saint is the one to speak up. "Can't we all learn?"

"Sure." Logan shrugs. "I guess we have to balance the workload you currently have on the books with this new stuff coming in. Janey?"

I nod. "We have a master calendar for the center. Why don't we overlay the stunt academy's stuff and figure it out?"

"Cool, cool." Logan detaches his computer. "As a side note, my brothers are really looking forward to meeting you all. As soon as they finalize their travel plans, I'm scheduling a big housewarming party at my place."

"Sorry, Saint. His supermodel sister is out of the country for the next few months." Bishop jokes.

I've been around men my entire career, and I know

all about the teasing they like to do—especially when it comes to little sisters—but hearing someone do it with Saint is a gut punch.

Everyone stands up, and I'm walking back to my office when I hear Barron say, "Hey Saint. What are you doing tomorrow night?"

"Nothing. Why?"

Linc walks up to the trio. "The four of us have tickets to the comedy club, and Betty has a coworker she thinks you'll like."

Oh god. Kill me now.

I hightail it out of there before I can hear Saint's answer. It stands to reason as the only single man here that the guys—or more to the point their ladies—would try to fix him up, but I don't have to be witness to it. I know someday soon a lucky woman will catch his eye, and I'll have to deal with that when it comes, but the longer I can keep my head in the sand, the better.

I power through another weekend alone by playing with the dogs, cleaning the house and the office, binging a new show on Hulu, and finishing Shay Marie's newest romance novel. Until Saint came to town, I don't think I realized how much time I spend alone. Of course, now that Kemp is shacked up with Mari, the last six months I've been mostly solo.

Speak of the devil—Kemp walks into my office and shuts the door. "We have a problem."

"We do?"

"Did you and Saint hash shit out?"

I shrug. "I mean, kind of. Why? I thought things were better in the office?"

He slides his hand down his face and tugs on his beard. "They are, but transitioning from military to civilian life doesn't seem to be going well for Saint, and Karden wants to host an intervention of some sort."

An intervention? That's hilarious. People like us don't do interventions.

Snorting, I wipe the smile from my face when Kemp turns his glare on me. "Oh god, you're serious?"

"His drinking is out of control, LaVey. I guess he went out with the guys to a comedy club Saturday night and was tossing them back. There's tension between him and his sister, which translates to tension between him and Karden." Kemp laces his fingers behind his head and stretches his chest as he paces small circles in my office. "Karden's prepared to deal with this one-on-one, but wonders if our collective experiences would help."

Shaking my head, I throw my pen down and lean away from my desk. "We aren't in the military anymore, Kemp, and we're not his supervisors, mentors, or NCOs. We can't tell him how to live his life."

"No, but we can tell our friend he's fucking up."

I close my eyes. "I can't do that, and you know it."

Kemp grits his teeth. "We've stood up a combat vet PTSD program here at the VKC. Although we're not therapists, we've received basic training to identify the symptoms. He's spiraling, Janey, and he's refusing to acknowledge it. Lots of guys get a couple of therapy sessions upon separating. Karden did a handful, Logan's finishing up now, and Bishop probably has a few more months, but Saint blew off his VA appointment, and apparently hasn't even filed his disability paperwork. He stopped looking for a house, and all signs point to..."

Don't say it.

Please don't say it.

The idea alone is enough to break my heart.

Licking my lips, I shake my head again. "An intervention is a bad idea. If you think he's not dealing with shit now, back him into a corner and see how bad it gets."

"That's what I was thinking."

I sigh. "He talked to me about Sylvie when we went out after his BBQ. Maybe he'll talk to me again?"

"I honestly think you're the only one he will talk to."

"Fuck me," I mutter, scared to death that I'll make things worse by confronting it with him. "I'll talk to him."

"Tonight," Kemp implores.

Nodding, I stand up and come around my desk. "Where is he?"

"He's in the yard."

I walk into the training arena and watch him run one of our clients through a series of recalls and corrections. He's always been an excellent trainer, and has a way about him that dogs respond to.

Women too, if I'm being honest. Behind closed doors,

I had no problem letting him take control of me, and he always made sure I enjoyed it.

As they finish up their session, I wave to the client as they walk past me with their golden doodle in hand, and stop next to Saint. "How's it going?"

He arches his brow while wrapping up one of the extra long leads. "Fine."

"What are you doing tonight?"

Saint stops what he's doing and faces me head on, his body inches away from mine. "Nothing. Why?"

My mouth falls open and I hesitate, my thoughts and words all scrambled up. Damn this is awkward. "I was thinking we could grab pizza and talk."

"Pizza?" He glances around and brings his eyes back to me, suspicion furrowing his brow. "A couple of slices between *friends*?"

"Something like that." I take a step back, needing a bit more breathing room between us. "I'll order from Mama Napoli. Do you remember where I live?"

"Yeah."

"Seven o'clock? You can bring Luce."

"I'll grab some beer."

"Let's skip the beer tonight."

The tip of his tongue pokes at his wolffish incisor as he slowly nods his head. "Okay."

Three hours later, Macha alerts me to someone in my driveway. I open the door in time for Luce and Macha to greet each other while Saint grabs the pizza from the delivery driver. "I was going to pay for that."

"I got it." He walks into my house, setting the food down on the counter separating my kitchen and living room while I unleash Luce. "Last time I was here, I neglected to tell you how much I like your decor. It reminds me of the cabana we stayed in at the resort in Santa Fe."

My heart jumps into my throat. I'm surprised he's bringing up our past. I kind of thought we'd silently agreed to pretend like it never happened.

"Uh, yeah."

"Plates?" He continues moving as if he didn't just dump a steamy pile of unaddressed shit in the middle of my living room floor.

"Top right cabinet."

He grabs them, and flips open the pizza box lid. "This looks good."

"Best in town." I reach into the refrigerator and pull out a couple of glass bottles of Coke.

"Holy shit. Where'd you get those?"

"There's a taqueria a couple of blocks away that stocks Mexican Coke and Jarritos. Every time I see them, I think of the time you made us try it while on that TDY in San Antonio."

"I had no idea you were thinking of me so often,

Janey." Saint takes a big bite of his slice, completely at ease with me for the first time in years, and flirting like he used to when no one was around.

Or he's faking it.

Either way, it's throwing me off my carefully rehearsed game.

"Okay." I grab a plate and two slices and take a seat on a stool at the breakfast bar.

"So, you want to talk to me about my drinking and self-destructive behavior?"

I pause with the slice to my lips. "What?"

"Come on, Janey. I know you better than anyone, and I figure you invited me here tonight for one of two reasons. One, the guys told you I made an ass out of myself Saturday night and they are worried about my drinking. Or two, you heard that I was talking all night to the nice woman they paired me up with—about you."

The blush hitting my cheeks clues him in. "Oh, you didn't hear that part?"

"What did you say?"

Saint arches his brow. "Do you really want to know?"

I take a big bite and chew thoughtfully while trying to calm the dread brewing in my belly. Now is the time for us to air out all the bullshit from our past. It's going to suck, but it has to be done. "That depends. How many times did you use the word 'bitch'?"

The smirk on his face falls, and he sets his slice down on the plate. "Why would I use the word 'bitch' when talking about you?"

I scoff, wishing we were drinking, because I really don't want to have this conversation sober. "It doesn't matter, Saint. Whatever you said, I'm sure you were right."

"It does matter, Janey. It matters to me."

VETERAN
K9
TEAM
REPORTING
FOR DUTY

Chapter 9
Saint

I grab the stool and move it aside so I can stand closer to Janey. "Why on earth would you think I have a bad word to say about you?"

"Oh, I don't know," she scoffs. "Maybe because the last time we saw each other I ran out on you in the pre-dawn light?"

"Yeah, that sucked." I stare down at the scar on her left cheek that mars my beloved freckles, my gut twisting with renewed anger. Dammit, I wish I had been there for her when she needed me. I would have put that douchebag in the ground. He never would have made it to trial and wouldn't be serving time now. "But I backed you into a corner with what I said. It wasn't fair to ask you to marry me when you weren't in love with me."

"It wasn't that." She shakes her head and stares down at her half-eaten slice.

"What was it then?" My fingers itch to push her short blonde locks back from her face.

"I'd just pinned on Sergeant First Class and was in the process of moving back to Georgia. My first shot at NCOIC of a battalion and I couldn't derail my career for a life with you."

I shake my head. "I never asked you to sacrifice your career. Nothing remotely close to that came out of my mouth. All I did was tell you I was in love with you and I wanted to marry you."

"I know." She closes her eyes, her voice barely above a whisper. "But if I had told you I loved you back, then where would the conversation have gone?"

All the air rushes out of my lungs. "Did you love me too?"

A rogue tear slips down her cheek.

Holy shit.

Fucking hell.

Are you kidding me right now?

Gently, I cup her cheek and turn her face to me, despite her keeping her eyes closed. "Did you love me too?"

"Yes," she whispers.

I'm not exactly sure what the tension in my chest is right now. Is my heart breaking again, or is it beating for the first time in three years?

"Open your eyes, Janey."

She does, her blue-green irises shining with unshed tears.

"Why didn't you tell me?"

"What would have been the point? I wasn't going to

change anything I had going on, and then it would have been lingering out there between us."

"It was lingering anyway." I softly swipe my thumb over her lips. "You should have told me. We could have figured something out. I'd waited seven years for you at that point. I would have waited a few more."

"Don't do that." She shakes her head and scrambles off the stool, taking several steps away from me. "Don't be nice to me, Saint. You're supposed to hate me."

"Why?"

"Because I hate myself for what I did to you, and to me."

"I've never hated you, Janey, but I've been plenty pissed at you." I glance around her living room, trying to formulate my words. "You went radio silent and shut me out, and then that douchebag hurt you, and you didn't let me in. I wanted to be the one who was there for you, and for a long time I was angry at Kemp for being there when I couldn't be."

Silent tears stream down her face. "Everything about Georgia that second time was fucked up, and I didn't know how to stop things once they went bad. It piled into a giant ball of shit and I felt stuck. None of it should have happened, and I was so embarrassed it did that I didn't want anyone to know, including Kemp, but especially you."

I walk toward her, grabbing her hands when she puts them up to warn me back, and pull her into my chest. Wrapping my arms around her, I simply hold her until she's sagging against me, her tears soaking through my cotton T-shirt.

"I heard the rumors, so I won't ask you to relive it by rehashing the details for me. Just know, if you had called, I would have dropped everything to be there for you."

"I know you would have, which is exactly why I never called. I didn't deserve your comfort then, and I don't deserve your pity now."

"I don't pity you. I'm angry for you."

"Well, I don't deserve that either." She pushes me back gently and wipes her cheeks. "We're here to talk about you, so how the hell did we end up talking about me?"

"Because when you look at the story of my life, it is about you."

"Dammit, Saint!" she barks and stamps her foot while clenching her hands at her sides. "This would be so much easier if you just called me a fucking bitch and got it over with."

"Fine!" I bark back. "You're a fucking bitch."

"Thank you," she says sharply.

"You're welcome," I answer with the same bite to my voice. We stare at each other for what feels like an eternity, years of emotions running through my body.

I love this woman.

I hate this woman.

I want this woman.

This woman makes me nuts.

It's never been sunshine and roses with Janey. She's never made it easy. Only when we stole time to be together was it perfect. That's the feeling I've been chasing for ten years. Those stolen moments when everything was easy.

It's the feeling I want infusing my soul forever.

Smiles slowly creep onto our faces. The next thing I know, we're laughing with two hyper-aware dogs between us. I stroll over to the couch and plop down on the seat. Luce shoves her head in between my knees to demand attention. I stroke her head and neck, feeling lighter than I have in months. Tiptoeing around each other with a million things left unsaid wasn't working, but this feels right—like unloading a fifty-pound rucksack at the end of a twenty-mile hike. Janey wasn't only my occasional lover, when she wasn't my boss, she was my friend and confidante. The person I would call once or twice a month and talk to for hours on end about life. We've been both friend and lover when we're geographically separated; why can't we be both here and now?

"Can you explain to me how the only two women in this world I care about refuse to let me be there for them?"

Janey plops down on the other side of the couch, pulling her knees up underneath her with Macha at her side. "I don't know, Saint. I never wanted to hurt you, so I thought pushing you away was the best for both of us. As far as your sister goes, have you and Sylvie talked yet?"

"No. I've been thinking about taking off, maybe grabbing a contractor job overseas or something to keep me busy."

"You can't leave." She grabs a pillow and clutches it to her chest. "You just got here and your family is here."

"I can't stay here with things the way they are. There's a lot of shit for me to fix, and for the life of me, I can't figure out how to."

Janey chews on her lip, staring at the seat cushion between us. "I think, maybe you need to let the past be the past. Neither of you can fix what has happened, and you can't be angry at each other for the choices you made. You have to draw a line in the sand and choose to have a new relationship from now on, damn the past."

I think through her words and nod slowly. She's right, but not just about Sylvie, about her and I. "That might work."

"People care about you, Saint. The guys care about you." She hesitates. "And so do I."

I side-eye her. "I know it."

"Then you also know that transitioning out of the military is hard, even when you have a group like us to come home to. You need to make and keep those VA appointments. They'll help. Plus the Army owes you fucking disability, so don't you dare turn your back on it."

I grin. This is the Janey I remember. The NCO outside of the bedroom who looks after her troops. She's a mother hen, whether she likes that title or not. "All right. I'll call them tomorrow and go to my appointments."

"Good. Now, let's talk about the drinking."

I look down into Luce's soulful, brown eyes, a little embarrassed about how I have conducted myself over the last couple of weeks. "It's already handled."

"It is?"

"Yeah, after Saturday night I took a hard look at myself. Our parents were alcoholics, so I come by it honestly. But until the last couple of weeks, I've been too busy to let it get this bad. It's a slippery slope, and me and my sister have to be honest with ourselves about it. I decided Sunday morning I wasn't going to drink for a while to make sure I have it under control."

"Then why did you offer to bring beer over tonight?"

"You invited me for pizza. What else was I supposed to bring?"

"Well, now you know there are other options." She straightens her leg, her toes close enough for me to touch.

I grab her ankle and pull her foot into my lap, just like I did years ago during our stolen moments when we'd hang out as man and woman, not colleagues. "You know me, Janey. When I set my mind to something, I make it happen. In the Army, I accomplished everything I said I would accomplish in the timeframe I said I was going to, except for making you fall in love with me. But, according to what you said fifteen minutes ago, maybe I accomplished that too?"

The blush that hits her cheeks followed by an eye roll makes me more happy than it should. There's still a lot of ground to cover between us, but I'm not giving up. Not now when I'm more than a little sure we finally have a shot at something real.

"Still cocky," she murmurs.

"Confident, not cocky. Remember?"

"I remember everything."

"Yeah, me too."

We stare at each other while my fingers dig into the arch of her foot and slowly work their way up her calf. Her breathing hitches as she reluctantly pulls her leg back and stands up. "Did we cover everything?"

I watch her walk into the kitchen, open up the pizza box, and toss a couple of slices into her toaster oven. Slowly, I stand up and follow her, waiting until she's done washing her hands and turning to face me. "Remind me of the deal with all of us and the VKC."

"What do you mean?" She leans back against the kitchen sink.

"We're partners, right?"

"Yeah. I mean, between Logan and I, we own the land and the buildings and lease them back to the center. But as far as any profit after expenses from the day-to-day operations—and eventually any income we get from the renters at the Pet Plaza—it's split between the nine of us. Right now it's not much, but eventually we should all be getting a nice quarterly dividend check. It'll take a couple of years to get there, but..." Janey rambles, and I'm amused by her focus on the money. If I wanted to make hand-over-fist cash, I'd have taken an overseas contractor job in a hostile location with hazardous duty pay—not come here to establish a home.

"Okay. But, we're partners, right? Not boss and employee?" I step into her space until she has no choice but to tilt her head back to look up at me.

She grips the edge of the counter, her elbows back

and breasts thrusted forward, and licks her lips. "We're partners."

"Then you've run out of excuses as to why we can't be together. Agreed?"

"I—" her blue-green eyes flash with heat "—guess so."

"So now, when I ask you out, if you say no it'll be because you don't want to date me. Fuck rank and file, and fuck the guys' perceptions of you or me or us as a couple. This time, if you say no, it's because you don't want me—but understand this Janey, it will be the last time I ask." I lean forward and kiss her forehead before taking a few steps back. "Pizza's ready."

Confusion furrows her brow, but she shakes herself and turns to the toaster oven. "Right."

For the next half hour, we eat our pizza, drink our Cokes, and talk about Spring City. The tension between us melts quickly, and I'm feeling better than I have in months. I have a plan that I'll launch tomorrow. By the end of this week, my world will be whole, or it will have completely imploded.

But, one way or another, constantly living in a state of unknown will be over.

Janey and Macha walk me and Luce to my truck. I'm sure she's confused because I haven't made a move on her, but done are the days of sneaking around. We're going to do this right or not at all.

I open my door and give Luce the command to jump into my truck. "I'm going to be late tomorrow, but I'll have Karden cover me."

"Okay."

"I'm telling you as my partner, Janey, not my boss."

She grins. "Okay."

"What are you doing Friday night?" I ask casually as I slide into the driver's seat. The words are breezy, but my heart is in my throat. If she tells me no, I don't know what I'm going to do.

"Going out with you, I hope." She leans her forearms through the open window of my truck door.

I flick my incisor with the tip of my tongue and nod. "Good answer. I'll pick you up at seven."

As soon as I walk into Karden's house our eyes lock. Things have been tense, but I give him a tilt of my chin and an easy smile.

"What's up?" He mutes the TV.

"Not much. Where's Demon?"

"Taking a bath."

"Cool." I plop down on the couch next to him. "Can you cover anything I have tomorrow morning at the center?"

"Sure. Why?"

"I'm taking Sylvie out for breakfast and fixing this."

Karden's breath comes out in a whoosh of relief. "Thank god because I fucking hate this."

"Me too, man. I'm sorry shit has been strained

between us and that I've been a self-destructive asshole, but I'm going to make it right. Promise."

"I think she's ready too." He slides his hand down his face. "We talked about it again tonight."

"Perfect." I bump his shoulder with my fist and stand up, stopping at the door to the basement where I'm bunking until I find a place to live, before glancing over my shoulder. "If I haven't said it, I'm thrilled that my best friend is the man who makes my sister happy. You were already family, and I can't think of one man I'd rather protect and love her than you."

Nodding, Karden turns off the TV. "Thanks, man. I appreciate you saying that."

"See you in the morning."

I don't see Karden in the morning, but I do run into Sylvie in the kitchen as she pours me a cup of coffee. "Hey."

"Good morning." I take the mug from her. "Want to have breakfast with me?"

She grins. "I haven't told you yet, but we found a diner here that rivals Ma's back home."

"Heart attack special?" I raise my brow in hope.

"Pot roast with gravy, scrambled eggs, rye toast, country hash browns, and dollar size pancakes."

"Fuck yeah." I chuckle. "I'll grab my keys."

Twenty minutes later we're sitting in a booth with two heaping plates of down-home cooking. "I was hoping we could clear the air this morning," I say around bites.

She nods, a forkful raised to her lips. "I'd like that."

"I love you, but I'm tired of apologizing for leaving

you all those years ago. I think you know how I feel, but maybe I've been asking for forgiveness in the wrong way over the years. If I could do it over, I would have done things differently."

Sylvie shakes her head and reaches across the table for my hand. "Don't apologize anymore. I love you, I've always loved you, and I'm sorry I've been a brat all of these years. You've gone above and beyond trying to take care of me from afar, doing the best you could for me while also taking care of yourself. Back then, I was too immature to understand that, especially when all I really wanted was for you to come home. But that wasn't fair either, because I certainly did not make it easy when you did come home. I think my anger was the only thing keeping me going most days. Bitchy Sylvie became part of my persona at the bar, and it wasn't until Karden brought me here that I realized I could change that—new people, new me, you know? When you came home, I learned that I didn't know how to be anything other than bitchy, bratty Demon with you. I don't want to be that person anymore. I forgive you. Can you forgive me?"

I grab her left hand with my right, our fingers curling around each other with our thumbs pointed toward the sky. Thumb wars. We used to play it all the time as kids, and if there is a perfect way for us to make a pact to bury the past, this is it. "I love and forgive you. Can we let the past be the past and move on?"

"Yes." She squeezes my hand and moves her thumb over mine.

But I can't just let her win, so I pull my thumb and

round over the top of hers. We do this back and forth until we're laughing and genuinely battling for dominance. Finally, I let her pin my thumb, and she squeals in triumph.

We return to our plates of food, but I have one more topic to broach before we're done. "One last thing."

"Yeah?" she says with a mouthful of pancake.

"I'm leaving the house and the bar in Rizona to you to deal with. Do whatever you want, but if you decide to sell and want me to go down there with you to clean up the properties and say goodbye, I'd be happy to do so."

Demon's eyes go down to her plate. "I've been thinking about that a lot the last few weeks. I think it would be therapeutic for us to do it together. Now that I'm here, I never want to go back."

"Whenever you want to go, let me know."

"We should probably go before school starts."

I set my fork down and stare at her. "You're going to school?"

A slick grin takes over her face. "Just a few general education classes this summer. I have an appointment with a counselor next week to discuss degree tracks, but I think I want to go medical. Maybe med tech, or radiology, or physical therapy—something like that."

"Fuck me, Demon. I'm so proud of you." The smile on my face could power a small nuclear arsenal. My heart swells with pride and love for my sister, now that our future is no longer overshadowed by pain and guilt.

"I'm not in school yet." She blows me off with a giggle.

"Doesn't matter."

"I was thinking about the bank account—" she hedges.

"It's yours. Use it to go to school full time." My mind races. "Actually, we should look to see if you can use my GI Bill for tuition, and—"

"Shut up, you big goon." She smiles. "I was thinking we should use that money to do something together. Like, buy an investment property or start a side hustle or buy and restore one of those vintage muscle cars we used to drool over as kids. Whatever, as long as it is something we spend time enjoying together."

Exhaling a deep breath, I nod. "That sounds perfect, Demon."

VETERAN
K9
TEAM
REPORTING
FOR DUTY

Chapter 10
Janey

It's late Friday afternoon when Saint stops by my office before heading out for the day. "See you in a few hours?"

"Yes." It's no secret he's taking me out. He didn't broadcast it, nor did I, but I overheard Bishop ask him this morning what he was doing tonight and he replied plainly, *"I'm taking Janey out."* If that news spread, none of the guys have said anything to me, which I guess means I've been worried about nothing for the last ten years.

He glances around the open bay behind him and lowers his voice. "Wear a skirt tonight."

"What?" A light blush hits my cheeks. This man has explored every inch of my body, and yet this makes me bashful and giddy?

"In the ten years I've known you, and the few times we've snuck around, I've never seen you in a skirt. Wear one tonight. This is a date, after all."

"I'm not sure I own a skirt."

"Make it a dress. I don't care, as long as I can see your legs." He waggles his brows playfully and leaves without saying another word.

Ten minutes later, the anticipation of going on an actual date with Jacob Santiago has me shutting down my computer and stuffing it in my bag.

"You ready to go, Macha?" I stand up and grab my bag, an uncharacteristic urge to primp making me anxious.

I want to look nice for our date tonight.

I want to look good for Saint.

Not once in all the years I've known him has he ever made me think he found me less than utterly desirable, and that was in ACUs with mud and dog slobber on me, or at the bar wearing jeans and a plain T-shirt, or naked and underneath him.

I'll admit, I like him best naked and on top of me too. That was when I felt I could be the most vulnerable, not because I literally was, but because of the way he cared for me in that state. With Saint, I've always felt safe. Too bad I wasted so many years worrying about the perceptions and pitfalls of being a woman in a man's world. Maybe if I had followed my heart back then, we'd be in a much better place now.

Rifling through my closet, I find a summer dress I bought five years ago. I giggle, because looking at it now, I remember when and why I bought it. I was at Target, of all places, when Saint texted me and suggested we take a four-day pass and meet somewhere in between Washington and Georgia. When I saw the frilly flowery thing I felt inspired, but we never could make that trip work, so I never wore it for him.

Man, I completely forgot this was in my closet. I'm curling my hair and contemplating the scar on my face when the front doorbell rings.

"Hi." I open my door.

Saint holds a bouquet—a garden variety of daisies and mums and roses—and smiles. "Hi yourself."

"You brought me flowers." I state the obvious.

"Well, you've never allowed me to give them to you before."

"They're beautiful."

He looks me up and down, smiling at my bare legs and ankle boots. "You're beautiful."

"Come in so I can put these in water." Blushing, I take the flowers from him and turn to the kitchen, slightly thrown off by the formality of a first date with a man that I've known for a decade. While the number of secret getaways can be counted on one hand, we always used our time wisely during those long weekends, enjoying each other as much as humanly possible. But he's right, I never welcomed any sweet tokens someone else could recognize as a romantic gesture. That didn't stop him from sending me notes—electronic and old-fashioned pen and paper. Then he bought me a physical gift the last weekend we were together—a silver and turquoise pendant that I'm wearing right now on a long chain that disappears under the bodice of my dress. "Where are we going tonight?"

"It's a surprise."

"You always said you were in control when it's just the two of us, so I suppose you expect me to let you lead tonight?"

"Absolutely. I'm taking you out." He leans down and kisses my left cheek. "You are finally mine to treasure openly."

Heat rushes through my veins at his words, and I stare up at him through my lashes. "Are you sure you want to go out?"

He grins and takes a step back. "Yes. I want you walking and sitting beside me, hand-in-hand, for the whole world to see."

"This is a public claiming?"

"Yes."

Biting my lip, I nod my understanding. "Okay. Let's go."

Saint escorts me to his truck with his hand on my back, and we hold hands while driving across town and up the mountain pass to a cute little winery off of Highway 24. I've never been here before, but I've driven past it and have always wanted to check it out.

While waiting for our table, Saint holds my hand and leans down to whisper in my ear, "You really do look beautiful in that dress."

"I'm glad you like it. I bought it years ago—for you."

"Really? When?"

"That time we tried to get a weekend away in Sioux Falls. I happened to be shopping at Target when we were texting about it, and this dress seemed like the perfect sexy surprise considering I've never been big on lingerie."

We're shown to our table which has a bench seat. Saint motions for me to sit down before sitting next to me so we are hip to hip versus across from each other. Our seating arrangement screams we are a couple, and for the first time I am more than okay with it.

I have to be, because I don't want to fuck up the opportunity Saint's offering me to mend our past and walk into a future—together.

"Do you want wine?" Saint asks.

"No, I'm good with seltzer water."

"We have great flavored seltzer waters and home-made ginger ales here. We infuse them the same way we infuse our meads and wines, so it's like getting a bubbly nonalcoholic version of some of our homemade concoctions," the server chirps.

"That sounds perfect. Bring me your favorite flavor." I nod.

"Two." Saint turns to me once the server walks away. "You can have wine; it's not going to bother me at all."

"I'd like to do this with you. Honestly, I probably drink more than I should. Why not go a few weeks or a few months without and see how it feels?"

He leans forward and kisses my temple, sliding his hand on top of my knee underneath the table. "I like being able to touch in public."

"I like it too."

Saint whispers in my ear, "I can't wait to do all the other things I want to do to you in public."

A mischievous grin spreads across my lips. "Are you telling me you have a kinky side?"

"Baby, I have ten years worth of fantasies to fulfill with you. You have no idea of the things I want to do."

"Maybe I have my own fantasies?"

"Well, we have a lifetime to fulfill them."

Looking into his eyes filled with undeserved love, the teasing tilt of his lips is too much. I shake my head and bring my eyes down to my lap. "I can't believe we're here right now. I'm surprised you're giving me another chance."

"We are giving us another chance."

The server comes and takes our orders, leaving us fruity little seltzer drinks that could also be called mocktails. I offer mine up as a toast. "To the first of what I hope are many dates."

Saint clinks my glass and says nothing, the smile on his face saying everything. Over the years I've kept a wall up, treating our times together as fun secret getaways, completely unwilling to fall for his charms—even though, deep down, I was under his spell from day one. Over the last week, I've dismantled those walls by telling myself he deserves nothing less than all of me.

Could he use it against me and break my heart? Absolutely.

But a life with him is worth the risk.

"How did your conversation with Sylvie go?"

"It went really well. We're letting go over our past hurts and starting our adult relationship. We're looking for a project to do together, nothing as aggressive as a bar, but maybe a car, or a fix-and-flip rental property—something silly like that. Any project where we spend time together and invest the money that I saved for her—which is now our money."

"That sounds amazing."

"I'm pretty excited about it. I lost the house that I had a deposit on, so I'm going to have to restart that process next week. My realtor already found me a few places to check out."

"You should buy my house," I say without thinking.

He arches his brow. "Where are you going?"

I shake my head and put my hand on his. "I think I'm going to have a temporary shelter brought onto the property so I can be closer to the puppies. The more we get, the more on-site one of us should be, and it might as well be me since it's my land."

"Why temporary? Why not build something permanent that you want to live in long-term? If you build it on the back edge of the property, it could feel like home without being too close to work." He nods as the server puts our plates down and excuses themselves. Picking up his utensils, he cuts into his steak. "People like us spend our lives living in temporary situations, Janey. You should build yourself a home."

"I'm working through the logistics of it, but I can't

afford to build a new house while I'm paying on my current one." Not wanting to admit exactly how in debt I am with the VKC, I shrug and dig into my melt-in-your-mouth pot roast and mashed potatoes, a soft moan escaping my lips. "Oh god, this is good. You want a taste?"

His chocolate eyes turn molten as he slowly nods his head and accepts the forkful I offer him. "That is good."

We spend the next half hour eating and chatting like old friends. It's always been easy between us when there is no one else around, and the only time it wasn't easy was because of me.

While we're eating, music plays somewhere nearby. It's loud enough to recognize as a live band, but far enough away to not be distracting from this beautiful candlelit dinner.

"Do you hear it?" I pause in between bites.

He nods. "They have a sister property on the other end of the parking lot where they have live music. I thought we'd go there after this."

After finishing our meals and paying the check, we walk into a tavern with a row of motorcycles parked out front. It's slightly behind the highway-facing restaurant and winery, so I've never noticed it before. It's not something you see from the road. "You've only been here a couple of weeks. How on earth did you find this place?"

"I've driven around a lot—trying to stay out of Sylvie and Karden's space while figuring out my life—and heading up the mountain pass is a perfect escape. There are so many scenic pullovers to hike from, which has given me a lot of time to think." The band transitions from a faster rock-n-roll song to a slower country song. I believe they're playing "Austin" by Blake Shelton. Saint brings our intertwined fingers up to his mouth and kisses my hand. "Dance with me."

I can't dance, but I put a smile on my face and nod just the same. On the dance floor, Saint pulls me close, leading us effortlessly around the small space. "I had no idea you could move like this."

"I've been asking you to dance with me for years. Do you really think I'd ask if I didn't know what I was doing?"

"I thought you were looking for an excuse to hold me tight against your hard body."

"Well, there is that too." He winks, spinning me out and pulling me back to him before bending me backwards over his forearm and leaning down to kiss me chastely in front of god and country.

Publicly claiming it is.

We finish the song and the next before leaving the dance floor and walking to a bar table in the corner. Saint leans against the wall and pulls me into his body, my back pressed against his chest, his arms wrapped around my waist. His breath tickles the hair on my neck as I lie my arms over his. "Is this okay?"

"This is perfect." I turn my cheek, our lips within touching distance.

He smiles, but doesn't move in for another kiss. "Are you ready to get out of here?"

"Please."

Driving down the mountain pass, I assume we're going back to my place—the butterflies in my belly doing somersaults over the orgasms Saint will give me tonight—but am surprised when he pulls into the Last Stand Saloon's parking lot. "What are we doing here?"

"It's Betty's birthday. Everyone is here tonight, celebrating." He puts the truck into park but doesn't shut down the engine and turns in his seat to face me.

"This is a test," I state versus ask.

He nods. "I guess it is. We don't have to go in there, Janey, but I want to. I'd like to rip off the bandaid and make it known to our friends and family—no more sneaking around."

I turn in my seat to face him. "I have something to tell you before we go in there."

"Okay."

"It's about Hugo."

"Who is Hugo?" He shakes his head and grumbles, "You mean the douchebag?"

I chuckle sadly. "Yeah."

"What is it?"

"I never loved him." I bite my lip and look down at my hands. "We went out a handful of times, drank a lot, had sex a couple of times, and next thing I know I'm pregnant. He suggested we get married because it would be better for the baby. Two military parents, family pay and all of that, plus we'd get post housing, and being married would make sure we'd get joint assignments—again, for the baby. I was so freaked out and embarrassed about being pregnant, I said yes. I talked about it with no one—not even Kemp—before I did it. And then I spent the next couple of months avoiding the guys, trying to hide the pregnancy and marriage."

Saint meets my confession with silence. I look up to find him staring out the windshield at the neon lights on top of the bar, the expression on his face blank.

"I'm telling you this because I want you to know that despite everything that happened, I've only ever loved one man—and that man is you. If you want to walk in there with me on your arm, I'm more than happy to do it, because you're not only claiming me, I'm also claiming you."

Saint turns off the engine and exits the truck without saying a word. I'm so shocked, I sit and watch as he rounds the hood and opens my door. He reaches over me and unbuckles my seat belt. His big hands cup my thighs as he turns me in the seat to face him, pulling me forward to the edge of the cushion. I have no choice but to spread my thighs as he pushes his body between my legs.

He brings his hands up to cup my face, his thumb brushing over the scar on my left cheek. "I've only ever loved one woman too—and that woman is you. Let's get in there and tell the birthday girl congratulations, so I can get you home and underneath me again."

I lean forward and place my mouth against his, my lips parting and tongue poking out for a taste of him again. Saint takes immediate control as he always has, devouring me with firm lips and a slick tongue. I squeeze my knees around his hips, desperate to have him pull me closer, so I can feel his hardness grinding against my softness once again.

He pulls back, chuckling. "I've missed the way you respond to me, Janey."

"I've missed you, period."

VETERAN
K9
TEAM
REPORTING
FOR DUTY

Chapter 11
Saint

We walk hand in hand into the Last Stand and find the team at a couple of tables in the corner between the bar and the pool tables. Sylvie and Tess are working tonight, but it's early enough that they see us walk in. I wave to my little sister at the same time Bishop smiles and offers me his hand. "You guys made it."

"Wouldn't miss it." Earlier in the week, Barron told me about the celebration and that's when I told the team that if I came, it would be later. I had no intention of making my date with Janey a big deal, but I also had no intention of hiding it either. The guys were remarkably cool about it, with Kemp and Vale muttering something like *about goddamn time*.

I'm guessing because they knew where Janey would be Friday night, that's why they didn't invite her, which under any other circumstance would not be cool. Hopefully, she's not bothered by it, but if she is, we'll address it later. I mean, one reason she never got involved with me was because being the only woman in the unit was hard enough without reminding the rest of the men that she wasn't exactly one of us. Just as much of a badass K9 handler as the rest of us—maybe more—but also desirable, which she never wanted anyone to focus on.

"Want a beer?" Logan offers.

"Not tonight." I wave it away and look at Janey who also shakes her head. She drops my hand and moves away to give Betty a hug and wish her a happy birthday while I make eye contact across the pool table with Kemp who tips his beer in my direction. I guess someday I'll have a heart-to-heart with him, because if I'm honest, there were many years after he separated from the military and followed Janey here when I treated him with less than the respect he deserved. He took care of my woman when I couldn't, regardless if she wanted him to or not.

If nothing else, I owe him an apology.

I nod back and slap palms with Karden while my sister slips in behind me to give me a quick squeeze. "You made it."

"I did. How's your night, Demon?"

"Easy money. Puppy Love is playing tonight, so the crowd is good. Have you seen them yet?"

I shake my head. "I don't think so."

"Nanook's owner is in the band." Karden reminds me of the short redhead who works at the VA hospital with the goofy Husky.

Linc hands me a pool cue. "You're up."

I glance at Janey who nods at me from several feet away. "Okay, one game."

For the next forty minutes, I'm reminded why I separated from the Army and moved to Spring City, Colorado. Seven of the best men I've ever known—and the only woman I've ever loved—live here. Together we're building something important for our brethren and the military community at large. And to top it off, my sister is here—safe and happy at last.

Although tomorrow is never guaranteed, things are looking a lot better for me than they were a week ago, and I'm excited about my future.

Janey comes to stand next to me as Kemp sinks the eight ball. I put my arm around her and pull her into my side, placing a chaste kiss against her temple and whispering in her ear, "You ready to get out of here?"

"Very."

"Awww. It's like you missed me or something." I grin.

"You have no idea." She flashes me a teasing smile and places her hand possessively on my abs right above my belt.

I growl softly. "I'm pretty sure I have an idea, because I know how much I've missed you."

"Oh yeah? Guess you'll have to show me."

I shove the pool cue into Karden's hands. "I'm going to swing by the house and pick up Luce."

He nods, chalking the end of the stick and doing his best not to laugh. "Sounds good, man."

We say our goodbyes and walk out the door ten minutes later without a single glance back at them.

"Was that weird for you?" I ask Janey as we drive to Karden's house.

"It surprisingly wasn't. I think I got more looks about wearing a dress than I did about being with you."

"That's because, as you designed over the years, the guys don't see you as a girl, but as a badass leader and soldier."

"Do you think that will change now that they know we're together?"

Pulling into the driveway, I shake my head and put the truck into park. "No. If they see you differently, it's because they'll recognize you as mine, but that doesn't change who Janey is to them. You're still their partner, amazing K9 trainer, and small business owner." I pop open my door. "Be right back."

"Why don't you pack a bag?" she calls after me. "It's silly to pretend like you're not spending the weekend."

What she doesn't know is that I already have a packed bag waiting on my bed. "Okay."

Luce and Macha greet each other while I shut and lock Janey's door behind me. As soon as my bag hits the ground, she's on me, climbing my torso with her arms flung around my neck. I slide my hands underneath her dress, cupping her ass and tracing over the soft edges of her panties with my fingertips. She's always been a plain cotton kind of girl, and I'd be disappointed if she'd changed over the years.

I carry her through the house to the bedroom at the end of the hall. Unlike the night I passed out in her guest room, tonight I get to see Janey LaVey's bedroom with her muted colors and a southwestern blanket draped across the foot of her bed. Setting her on the mattress, I press one knee down between her legs and push the skirt of her dress up to her waist.

White cotton panties with little blue flowers on them equals absolute perfection. "You are the sexiest woman I've ever known."

"I'm so glad you don't need lingerie to find me desirable." She giggles, lifting up and pulling her dress over her head before lying back. That's when a silver and turquoise pendant slides from her breasts up to the hollow of her throat.

"Holy shit. I didn't realize you were wearing this tonight." I pick up the pendant, holding it between my thumb and forefinger, a flood of memories hitting me. We were at a Santa Fe artisans fair a few blocks from the hot spring resort. It was one of the few times we've walked around freely like a couple, and it was the moment I knew I needed a lifetime of it—sooner rather than later. We stumbled upon a young vendor who sold handmade jewelry, guaranteeing each pendant to be one of a kind.

As soon as I saw it, I knew Janey had to have it.

"I wear it all the time—always close to my heart."

"You really do love me."

Instead of an answer—not that I asked a question— she points to the wall at the foot of the bed.

I follow her hand to a dozen framed drawings and realize they are the ones I sent her over the years. "My doodles?"

"No, they are my doodles. You made them for me. They are mine."

"I can't believe you kept and framed them."

She slides her slender hands on my cheeks, turning my head back to her. "I kept everything, Saint. Every gift, every note, every email, and every text message. I have them all."

Any residual hurt infecting my heart disintegrates, and something unexpected flies out of my mouth. "Marry me, Janey."

Tears fill her eyes. "What?"

Shit. I didn't mean to say that, but I feel it in my heart and soul as strongly as I did the last time I said it. Time stops as we stare at each other, both of us searching for answers in the other's eyes.

"Yes." She nods, the tears spilling out. "I will marry you."

That's it. There are no more words to be said.

No more apologies.

No more regrets.

From this moment on, we're staring at our future. It is utterly surreal and way overdue as I kiss her with ten years of pent-up love and devotion.

She wraps her arms and legs around me and squeezes me tight. Maybe this doesn't feel real to her either, and she's trying to reassure herself that I'm really here.

I am here. And I'm going nowhere without her ever again.

Running my hand over her ribs, I cup her breast and flick open the front clasp of her bra. Although I've been touching and tasting her for nearly a decade, every time feels like the first time and tonight is no exception. With her, I've never felt hurried, because deep down I knew I wanted to memorize every minute.

Janey pulls at my shirt, sliding her hands between our bodies to attack the buttons. I pull back long enough to make quick work of removing my clothes, yanking off her booties in the process, and then spread out beside her, reacquainting myself with every inch of her perfect body.

"I really missed you," Janey whispers. "Not just the way you love my body, but I missed having you as my friend."

I slip my fingers between her legs, smiling as she arches up into my hand. "I'm here now, baby. Friends. Lovers. Partners. It's you and me forever."

She pulls my face down to hers and kisses me softly while staring into my eyes. "I didn't think I'd get forever."

"Me neither." I smile.

"Make love to me, Saint."

"I can do that."

Moving between her legs, I pull off her panties and push my hips between her thighs, my cock sliding between her slick folds for the last first time.

All of the other times were fun—practice for now— and although I knew I wanted forever, I also knew it wasn't the right time or place for us. But this time I'm claiming her as mine. No other man will ever touch her, look at her, or profess to love her again.

She's mine, finally, which makes this feel better than ever before.

Her body welcomes me like it always has, but the emotions between us amplify the sensations shooting up my spine as I pump my hips and slide the head of my cock slowly against her g-spot. "Fuck, you feel good."

"So, so good." She gasps and digs her fingers into my shoulders. We keep our eyes locked onto each other and I watch each emotion dance across her face. Gone is the trepidation she used to have with me. I always knew she was holding back—which, I suppose is also how I knew deep down that she was in love with me. She was always guarding her heart around me, a giant brick wall with cracks in the mortar that I could peek through but couldn't break down, which made me love her even harder.

Gone is that wall.

Staring back is a woman completely in love with me.

"I love you, Janey."

She smiles. "I love you so much, Saint. I always have."

"You're stubborn." I kiss her lips and pull her knee up, pushing in deeper. "It's one of the things I love about you."

"I'm glad you like a challenge." She moans as I thrust my hips forward with more force.

"Are you going to come for me, baby?"

"Yes." She arches her back. "Keep going... just like that."

The moment her cunt tightens around me, she tosses her head back and lets out a garbled cry. Her pussy throbbing around my cock is pure ecstasy, but I refuse to come yet. I give her a minute to ride out her climax before I roll us, putting her on top of me, the silver and turquoise pendant hanging perfectly between her bare breasts.

"Did you come?" She places her hands flat on my stomach and adjusts her hips, riding me slowly.

"Not yet, baby."

"We should talk about that."

"Okay?" I arch my brow.

"I'm not on the pill. I haven't been for three years." She bites her lip. "I also haven't had sex since—"

"Not once in three years?" I ask incredulously.

She shakes her head. "No desire to date, much less..."

I don't want to tell her about the rampage I went on before deploying a few weeks after finding out about her nuptials. Truthfully, I barely remember the weeks between my father's death and landing back in the sand-box. It was a drunken blur with nameless faces that I regretted as soon as it happened.

Not my finest hour.

"Do you want kids?" she murmurs.

The look on her face... Jesus, we have so much to talk about. I have no idea how she feels about the child she lost, but I have to imagine there's a residual sorrow in her heart that will never go away. Even if she wasn't in love with the douchebag—I refuse to give him a name—and the pregnancy was an accident, she was far enough along to have come to terms with the inevitability of having a child.

I cup her face. "I want everything with you. What-ever makes you happy, baby, I will give you. Do you want kids?"

"With you, I do."

Grinning, I swipe my thumb across her pouty lips plumped by my kisses. "You know, the first time we were together, I imagined you swollen with my child. It was just for a second, but I liked it all the same."

She rolls her hips, slowly riding me, picking up a rhythm that takes me back to fully hard and on the edge. "Well, I guess we know where we stand on the topic of you—"

"Coming inside you?" I grip her hips, thrusting up to drive home my point.

She hisses. "Yes."

"Yeah, we know where we stand. You're mine, I'm yours, and we're at the beginning of the rest of our lives." Quickening my pace, she leans back and places her hands on my thighs behind her ass. I press my thumb against her clit and rub small circles, her pussy quivering with another orgasm seconds before I come.

Janey collapses on my chest, her face nestled in my neck. I wrap my arms around her tightly and press a kiss to her cheek. "Love you Janey LaVey-Santiago."

"Am I hyphenating my last name?" she asks.

I shrug. "I don't know, baby. I just wanted to hear it out loud."

"If you're Saint, and Sylvie is Demon, what's my nickname going to be?"

"You're my Angel—" I kiss her temple and pull the soft wool blanket over us "—but you're also a temptress. The only woman I've ever been bedeviled by, but I wouldn't want you any other way."

"We have a lot to figure out." She slides her finger down my sternum to my belly button, her cheek resting against my pec.

I grab her hand and bring it to my mouth, kissing each fingertip. "Outside of putting a ring on your finger and a baby in your belly as soon as possible, we have all the time in the world to figure the rest of it out. No more deployments or PCSs—we're no longer working against a clock. I'm here, you're here, and everyone is happy for us. It's time to start the rest of our lives, Janey."

"I'm ready." She smiles up at me.

"Me too, baby. Me too."

VETERAN
K9
TEAM
REPORTING
FOR DUTY

Epilogue
Janey - Four months later

"I wanted to get married immediately, and would have been fine with a justice of the peace ceremony, but Saint wanted us to celebrate our union with our friends," I confess to Sylvie as she fixes the flowers in my hair. Sylvie is as much of a tomboy as I am, so we're hopeless at trying to glam me up. Actually, none of the women in my life are overly girly. Definitely not Cher, Mari, or Tess. I don't even think Betty or Brandi do their hair on a regular basis or wear a lot of makeup. Maybe Charity, but no, she's pretty down to earth too?

I guess that's why I like all of them so much. Low-maintenance, like me.

"Well, I'm happy you are doing it this way. I would've been very upset with you for denying me this day." Sylvie spins in her cocktail length bridesmaid dress. "I mean, when else will I wear a dress like this?"

"You and me both, chick." I glance in the mirror at myself wearing a summery off-the-shoulder white cotton dress with eyelet overlay that is more "meadow of flowers" than wedding. It suits me so much better than a heavy, traditional wedding dress. We are having a small wedding between the recently emptied building on the property—the one that Logan had built into a scene from his brother's upcoming movie, *After Sunset*, to train the dogs—and a giant outdoor tent laid over the freshly cut grass.

The building is the same one Cher and Vale were married in last October. The tent is because it's forecasted to be a perfect Spring City summer day. Two weddings on the property in less than a year—I never thought mine would be one of them.

Of the people assembled, only four are blood relatives. Sylvie is Saint's only living relative that either of them keep in touch with. No aunts, uncles, or cousins. I guess their parents alienated the rest of the family early on before moving to the middle of nowhere, Rizona.

My aunt Sally and my two cousins are the only family I have on my mom's side. I met my aunt when I was a kid, but she moved away before I was done with elementary school. We talk once or twice a year, if that, but don't have much in common. Honestly, I think she's still pissed that my grandfather, her father, left me this parcel of land—not that she'll admit it. The simple fact is, I was more of a daughter to him than she was considering he raised me practically by himself from the time my mom got sick until she died before my sophomore year of high school. I haven't talked to any of my half-brothers in fifteen years—my father, the sperm donor, was a world class philanderer—and didn't even think about inviting them.

Other than those four people, everyone else here is the family Saint and I adopted over the years, to include guys we've served with and an ex-Army, now deputy from Rizona who is thinking about moving here and joining the El Paso county sheriff's department. I met him last night, but I suspect I will be seeing a lot more of him because Saint rented him the travel trailer until he can get a job.

It's been a crazy couple of months.

"Are you ready?" Sylvie hands me a bouquet of wild-flowers.

"As ready as I'm going to get." I fidget with my skirt again.

"You look beautiful. My brother is going to eat his tongue when he sees you." Sylvie hugs me. "I'm so excited to have a sister-in-law."

"I want to thank you for everything. Today wouldn't be half as beautiful as it is if you hadn't made it your mission to glam it up."

Sylvie giggles and waves my compliment away. "Not me. It was the rest of the ladies, but especially Mari and Cher. My idea of romance is hot pink neon lighting."

I snort. "Yeah, me too."

"Let's go!" She pushes open the door of our one-bedroom bungalow we've built on my property. It's our temporary home while our four-bedroom stick-built permanent home is constructed on the northeast corner of my property. Logan loaned us the money to build the bungalow—which will replace the travel trailer the guys sack out in on occasion—so we could sell my house and put down the money to buy the plans and have our dream home built. Having a friend and partner with money does make things go a lot smoother, but we will pay him back in the end.

In lieu of high heels, because I've never worn heels over two inches in my life, I'm wearing a pair of light tan cowgirl boots with my dress. I follow Sylvie through the back door of the building where linen-draped tables, full dinner catering, a nicely stocked bar, a DJ, and a dance floor take over the otherwise blank slate. "Oh my god, this is beautiful."

"It cleans up really well. I guess Mari has all the connections," Sylvie says while marching me to the other side and another door, where I'm supposed to step out on a runner that leads through white folding chairs under a giant canopy tent to an altar—where hopefully Saint waits for me.

Kemp and Vale are standing at the door, grinning at me like a couple of loons.

"Ah, Janey. You look perfect." Kemp chucks me on the shoulder lightly.

Vale, who has his one-month old child strapped to his chest, grins. "A big frilly wedding dress wouldn't have matched your personality, but this is beautiful. Simple, classy, and pretty—just like you."

"Get out of here with the sappy talk." I snort, a light blush tinting my cheeks. "You guys better take your seats. We're about to get started."

"Actually," Kemp brushes imaginary lint off his Class-A suit jacket, "I'm here to walk you down the aisle."

"What?"

"Yeah, right after you got engaged, Saint pulled me aside for a talk. He thanked me for being there for you—taking care of you when he couldn't—and apologized for being an ass the last few years."

"He'd been an ass to you?" I'm surprised because Kemp never once complained about Saint.

"Yeah, but I knew why, so I didn't let it bother me. He said I was the closest thing to a brother you have, and he'd appreciate it if I was the one to give you away today." Kemp leans down and presses his forehead to mine. "You are my pain-in-the-ass little sister, after all."

I bite my lip and will back the tears. "I don't know what to say."

"You've said it many times over the last few years, Janey. We're family. We take care of each other, and we have each other's backs."

"Yeah." I can't say more or I'll start crying before the ceremony starts.

"Cari and I are your flower girls." Vale shakes a shiny tin bucket of flower petals at me.

I laugh—the tears I can't stop are a mixture of happy and grateful. "Oh my god, I hope somebody is videotaping this."

"Oh, you know the guys are." He grins. "I'll never hear the end of this, so I'm going to make it good. You know I wouldn't do this for anyone else."

"You'd do it for me and Mari when the time comes."

"I better be standing next to you when you marry Mari, asshole."

"Language." I point to the little one passed out cold in her Baby Bjorn.

"Shit. My kids don't stand a chance with me and Cher in the house." He waggles his brow.

"Kids?" I ask.

He grins sheepishly at the same time music starts to play and Sylvie pokes her head outside. "Time to go!"

First Sylvie walks out, then Vale and Cari—the chorus of hoots and hollers making me wish I was already up front watching the show—which leaves me and Kemp. I place my hand in the crook of his elbow and smile up at him.

He smiles back. "I'm thrilled you finally got here, LaVey. You deserve a man who treasures everything about you. Saint's been that guy for a long time. The two of you deserve to be happy."

"Thanks, Kemp." I lift up on my toes and press a kiss to his fuzzy cheek. "For everything."

"Always. I'm here for you."

We push through the door and the first thing I see is Saint with Luce and Macha lying at his feet, his eyes on me. He smiles softly, his gaze drawing me in to the point that no one else exists. It's like the first time I saw him and the rest of the crowd faded away. Kemp walks me down the makeshift aisle, shakes hands with Saint, and then presses a kiss to my cheek.

Saint takes my hand from Kemp, and we turn to face

the non-denominational pastor we met a month ago. Next thing I know, he's declaring us man and wife. "You may kiss the bride."

Saint's eyes sparkle as he pulls me into his arms. "Isn't this better than the JOP?"

"So much better." I press my lips to his, unable to hold back a second longer. He's mine, finally, after all of these years.

Our friends—the men I spent fourteen years around thinking I had to be a non-feminine, badass soldier in front of in order to be considered one of them—applaud us.

Karden stands next to Saint and gives me a friendly smile and nod of his head. "Congratulations, you two."

Sylvie claps her hands with a small bounce in her step. "Yay! Let's party."

"Time to celebrate, Mrs. Santiago." Saint takes my hand and we turn toward the wedding party, walking past them as we make our way down the aisle back to the building and reception.

I make eye contact with each member of my team as we pass them, thinking about Kemp's words from twenty minutes ago.

This is my family. We came from different parts of the country, bonded by camouflage, dog slobber, and a love for our fellow veterans. Maybe we're dysfunctional at times, but I couldn't have chosen better brothers and sisters to call my own.

And now I'm blessed to have the love of my life by my side.

We will always take care of each other, and anyone else that comes along too.

Our family is growing, and I can't wait to see what the next generation brings into our world.

I'm so thankful for my Veteran K9 Team.

VETERAN
K9
TEAM
REPORTING
FOR DUTY

Second Epilogue
Saint - 15 Months Later

"Where's Janey?" Kemp asks as he pours him and Vale a cup of coffee.

"She hasn't been feeling good lately. I told her to stay in bed today, and that we have it handled." I grab my mug and fill it up.

"She's been fighting something for a couple of weeks now, right?" He arches his brow and sips from his mug, sliding his eyes in Vale's direction.

I look up at the ceiling, trying to put all the pieces of the last month in order. We did the final walk-through on our new home four weeks ago and moved all of our stuff in—to include the shit we've had in storage for the last year—a few days after that. It's been buying appliances, unpacking, decorating, and arranging furniture ever since. "We've been working our asses off getting the house settled."

Vale nods. "Could be that."

"Do you think she's sick?" My clueless ass asks.

Kemp shrugs. "Are you feeling run down?"

"Not really."

"Has she taken a pregnancy test?" Vale pins me with a *do-I-have-to-spell-it-out-for-you* look.

"No..." All of their hints come crashing down on me at once. "Shit. I'll be right back."

"There he goes." Kemp chuckles as I run out of the office and down the quarter of a mile dirt drive separating our house from the center.

"Janey?" I bust through the front door and climb the stairs to the second floor. The bed is empty and I peek into the bathroom, finding Janey sitting on the toilet with a pee stick in her hand. "Baby?"

"Yep." She holds the stick up, two pink lines staring back at me. There's no emotion on her face, which scares the shit out of me.

I drop to one knee in front of her, placing my hands on the outside of her knees. "What's wrong?"

"I..." she sighs. "I was afraid I couldn't get pregnant, and now I'm afraid—"

"What are you afraid of?"

"We've been having unprotected sex for almost two years, Saint. What if I can't carry our child to term?"

"Why would you think that? Did the doctor say something?" We've made a couple of trips to her obstetrician over the last year, who told us everything looked good all things considered. Janey is almost thirty-five, but she's healthy and the doctor said she wasn't worried. Considering everything else going on, I hadn't realized this was affecting Janey so deeply.

Damn. I hate that this has been bothering her and she hasn't talked to me about it.

"No." She shakes her head. "Quite the opposite. She said my past trauma shouldn't affect getting pregnant or carrying to term, but I don't know. I guess I'm afraid of getting my hopes up."

"Baby, come with me." I guide her back to bed and stretch out beside her, wrapping my arms around her with my lips finding her temple, cheek, and lips. "Finding out that you're pregnant should be a joyful event, not something to fear for the next eight or nine months. The way I understand things, miscarriages are common in the first trimester, and there is nothing we can do to stop them. Let's make an appointment with the doc and go from there."

"You're right." She sighs, her body relaxing in my arms. "Let's not tell anyone until the second trimester, though. Just in case."

"Uh, I think that ship has sailed. I came running into the house like a bat out of hell just now because Kemp and Vale brought it up. Mari's due any day now, and Vale just found out Cher is pregnant—again. Between the two of them, they have baby batter on the brain."

"Shit."

"We don't have to confirm or deny anything, and I seriously doubt either of them will ask. Let's make an appointment and go from there. Okay?"

She looks up and gives me a small smile. "I love you, Saint."

"I love you more."

Three days later we're in the exam suite. I'm sitting beside Janey holding her hand while she's trussed up in a white hospital gown with her legs in stirrups. I'm no doctor, but the entire setup feels a little barbaric. Now the doctor is spreading cool gel on her belly and using a wand to take images of the baby.

And that's when we see what the doctor explains is a heart beat. But it's more than that. It's the shape of a head, arms, and legs, and a tiny beating blip on the screen that screams life. We stare at the moving image in silence as the oxygen in the room thins and I feel like I can't breathe.

"Holy shit," I mutter as Janey tightens her grip on my hand.

"It's much too soon to tell the sex, but from what I'm seeing here, you have a healthy implantation. You look to be about eleven weeks along. Congratulations." The doctor smiles.

"Eleven weeks?" Janey says, looking at me.

"Yeah. You're lucky you didn't get hit with major morning sickness in your first trimester. Only about one-third of women get the pleasure of skipping it. There's a possibility you'll get lucky and never have it at all." She uses a soft towel and wipes the gel off Janey's belly before removing her gloves. "Why don't you get cleaned up and then come to my office. We'll talk about what's next."

The doctor and her assistant leave the room. I take a step back and let Janey do what she needs to do, pulling on her clothes and tossing the gown in a giant bin.

Once she's standing, I pull her into my arms and hug her close. "Holy shit. How do you feel?"

"Eleven weeks." Janey shakes her head. "I'm almost in my second trimester."

"That's a good thing, right?"

"Yeah." She chuckles and rubs her face against my chest.

"What's so funny?" I pull back and frame her face with my hands.

"I'm having your baby." The smile on her face lights up the room.

"Yeah, you are." I kiss her possessively, every inch of the love I have for her radiating through my fingertips. "Let's get in there and find out what's next so I can get my babies home."

#

"Janey. I need you to tell me if this is straight or not." I yell from the stepladder I'm precariously perched on while trying to hang an embroidered quilt the team had made for the baby.

My woman stops in the doorway of our nursery. "Saint."

"Is it straight?"

"It's time."

"What?" I glance over my shoulder and lose my balance, dropping the heavy quilt and falling to my ass in the middle of the nursery.

"Are you okay?" Janey pants.

"What do you mean, it's time?"

She nods. "It's time."

I glance at her belly, my endorphins kicking in. If I broke anything in the fall, I'll deal with it later. "It's time."

Taking deep breaths, she turns and walks slowly down the hallway. "Can you grab my bag?"

"Yeah." I jump off the floor and run into our bedroom, grabbing our go bags and phone chargers. Janey is at the bottom of the stairs sliding her feet into slip-on shoes at the same time I rush through the house and into the garage, throwing our bags into the back while ensuring the dogs are good to go. Luce is nearly ten years old, and Macha is almost six, but I'll call the center and ask someone to come check on them anyway.

"You ready?" I pull up short beside Janey, sliding her phone into her leather knapsack.

"I think so. I'll make calls while you drive." I get her situated and drive carefully down our dirt road, wishing we could afford to have it paved so I could give my wife a comfortable ride.

Janey calls the hospital and the doctor first, and then she calls Sylvie. "We are a go."

I can hear Demon squealing through the phone before Janey puts it on speaker. "What do you need us to do?"

"Nothing right now."

"Actually, let Karden know I need him to check on the dogs before he leaves for the day," I say as I turn my big truck onto the highway.

"Okay. Will you give us your room number once you're settled?"

"Of course." Janey hisses and pushes her phone onto my lap. I hit the audio button and connect to the truck's speakers before offering her my hand. She squeezes with the strength of a thousand men, damn near crushing my bones.

"Got to go, Demon. I'll call you once we're settled." I glance over at my wife. "Fifteen minutes, baby."

Janey pants and nods. "I'm okay."

Once we pull up to the hospital, everything runs like clockwork. There's a valet to park my truck, and an OB nurse waiting with a helper manning a wheelchair. They whisk Janey and I up to the sixth floor and our private birthing suite. Honestly, I'm not sure we would have known about all of this if Tess wasn't a month away from giving birth herself. Logan, of course, will only accept top tier healthcare for his wife, which is ironic considering he takes himself to the VA on occasion.

I grab a spot near the window as the nurses get Janey settled in her bed, hooking up monitors to her arms and chest, with a baby monitor over her belly. The nurses come and go over the next twelve hours while we wait for Janey to fully dilate. As a man in this situation, I feel worse than helpless as I do everything within my power to comfort my wife. If I could take her pain away, I would, but I'm also smart enough to know that saying such meaningless words out loud might get me smacked by not only Janey, but any one of the female nurses running in and out of the room.

"Would you sit down, Saint," Janey sighs, her face a mask of utter exhaustion.

"I hate not being able to do anything for you." I kiss her hand and take the cool washcloth off her forehead.

"Yeah, me too." She motions to the TV in the corner. "Why don't you find us something to watch?"

I flip on the TV and surf channels for twenty minutes, nothing catching either of our attention. She's contracting every couple of minutes, and I swear I don't know how she's still conscious with the amount of pain I have to believe she's in. I know we want this, and I know we'll be rewarded with a beautiful baby boy when it's all said and done, but I'm not sure this was our greatest idea. Watching the love of my life go through this while I do nothing is pure torture.

The doctor walks in looking freshly scrubbed after a recent shower. Her put together facade grates on me, ironically. "I think we're close. How are you doing, Janey?"

"I'm tired."

"I bet. How are you holding up, Saint?"

"I'm fine."

"Stoic and smart enough not to complain, good man."

Janey chuckles. "He is a good man. We need to give him something to do."

The doctor slides on a glove and does another check, smiling and nodding at both of us. "Oh, he'll be busy holding his son very soon. Are you ready?"

Next thing I know, there is a flurry of activity. I stand by Janey's head, holding her hand and gritting my teeth as I watch something akin to combat fly through the room. Everyone has a job and is braced for battle as Janey pushes a beautiful, healthy, six-pound-fourteen-ounce boy into the world. The moment I hear my son wail from his perfect lungs, tears fall down my eyes. I learn down and kiss Janey's sweat soaked hair, muttering over and over again, "I love you. I love you. I love you."

They quickly clean and then lay Karson Jacob Miles Santiago on Janey's chest. I rest my head on the pillow next to her, my eyes bouncing between Janey and our son.

"He's beautiful." Janey half-sobs, half-laughs.

"He's perfect." I gently trace all ten fingers and toes.

"He's got your hair." She slides her fingers through the thick mop of black curls on his head.

"Hopefully, he'll have your eyes." I grin. "Can you imagine? Near black hair and blue-green eyes. He'll have all the girls chasing after him, just like his daddy."

Janey snorts. "Aren't you the cocky one?"

"Not cocky, baby. Confident that I'm married to a perfect woman, and we just made the best looking baby in the world."

Also by Kameron Claire

Want more **Witty** Tongues, **Wicked** Needs, & **Wild** Deeds?

Hollywood Lights (Pre-Order)

* Billionaire Romance *

Show Time (Securing Selyne)

Money Shot

Three Shot

Martini Shot

Long Shot

Veteran K9 Team

Military Romance

Mine to Cherish

Mine to Crave

Mine to Possess

Mine to Adore

Mine to Covet

Mine to Worship

Mine to Protect

Mine to Treasure

Hot Nights with the Boss

** Forbidden Office / Age-Gap Romances **

Dating the Boss

Flirting with the Boss

Teasing the Boss

Tempting the Boss

Rangers Football

** Sports Romance **

Play Action Fake

Quarterback Sneak

Personal Foul

Two-Point Conversion

Red Zone

Man to Man Coverage

Short Story Collections and Bundles

Animal Attraction 4-Story Collection

Vegas Nights 4-Story Collection

Last Stand Saloon 4-Story Collection

Instalove Bundle

Grayson Enterprises Series

Bedding the Boss

Enticing the Ex

Tempting the Teacher

Wedding the Widow

Exclusives and Sneak Peeks

Get exclusive stories, updates, sneak peeks, and special content only available to subscribers...

Join our Mailing List Today!

Sign Up Here

About the Author

 USA Today Bestselling Author Kameron Claire writes stories with witty tongues, wicked needs, and wild deeds. Her books emphasize strong female leads and the protective alpha males who know how to love and support kick-ass, take-charge women. Many of her books contain military veterans, boss babes, gentle but dominant men, and goofy K9 hijinks.

Find her everywhere via linktr.ee/kameronclaire
Signed Paperbacks and discounted eBook bundles are available exclusively on her store
Subscribe to the Witty, Wicked & Wild community and read all her books online for as little as $5 a month.